FATE OF THE WOLF

PACK LOYALTY

BOOK ONE

AMELIA SHAW

CHAPTER 1
ALLARA

I grimaced at the clock on the dashboard as I pulled up outside the bar I'd worked at every weekend for the past five years.

Late as always. Mick's really gonna kill me this time.

I jumped out of my car and slammed the door. The old rust bucket was reliable and got me where I needed to go, even if the aesthetics left something to be desired.

I ran through the back entrance, pulled off my woolen coat and dumped my bag in the small cupboard we had for employees, fumbling with my keys.

The bar wasn't one of those dive bars with only two lights bulbs that worked, but it wasn't a fancy two story place with a super-expensive menu, either.

It was warm and friendly, with an affordable menu. The locals considered it the perfect place to hang out after work, or on the weekends.

"Allara. You're late. Again," Mick called out to me, his tone dripping with sarcasm. "You're lucky I love you!"

I *was* lucky.

He really did love me, and as a wolf shifter without a pack... I needed a family. Mick was the only father figure I had in my life these days.

I threw him a grateful smile. "You know I'll make up the time at the end of the night."

He tossed me a chef's apron and I caught it one handed, trying to suppress a groan. He liked us to wear them on nights when more beer got spilled than drunk.

Football finals.

That was tonight! Shit.

"The place is already half-full, so..." He clapped my shoulder with a heavy hand. "Better get out there."

I tied the apron around my waist, covering my new jeans. It seemed a bit of a waste to wear them at work, especially since no-one could really see me from the waist down behind the counter anyway. But... new jeans. I couldn't resist trying them out.

"Thanks, Mick."

I walked through the kitchen, tossed a quick hello to our chef Louise, then strode out to take my place behind the bar. My heart was still pumping from the rush to get here, but my body was beginning to hum pleasantly, my hips swinging to the music playing over the bar's speakers.

I might whine and moan about having to work weekends, but mostly, it was all show. I really didn't have anything else I'd rather be doing. This place, and the people who worked here, had become a home to me. I enjoyed my nights here and there were definitely worse jobs. Even on nights like this, with the rowdy football crowd making extra work and noise.

I grabbed a hair tie from around my wrist and threw my long hair up into a high ponytail. On football nights, the place got stupid hot and people flooded in non-stop until the early hours of the morning. Working the bar on a busy Saturday was basically the equivalent of a free gym workout.

"Hey Tammy!" I called out to the other bartender, who was shaking a tumbler and pouring what looked like a cappuccino cocktail mixture into two glasses.

Ooh, fancy.

"Hey Allara," she called back with a wide grin. "How's it going?"

Tammy was a nice chick, the ideal bar partner for this sort of place. We worked hard—probably *too* hard—but I think she enjoyed the rush as much as I did. The bar was busy enough to warrant hiring a third bartender, but thanks to the fact that Tammy and I could run an eight-hour shift on our feet, Mick didn't need anyone else.

Being a wolf shifter meant I had a fast metabolism and more strength than a non-paranormal human. I could work hard without really feeling it physically. Tammy was driven by pure energy. There was no paranormal in her, but she still worked like a trojan—I assumed, just because she could. She was awesome.

"Hey. Can I get two brewskies?" a guy called out, shaking me out of my train of thought. He threw a twenty on the bar in front of me.

I stopped a sigh from escaping just before I politely plastered on my "work face".

No rest for the wicked, or so the saying went.

"Of course! Can I get you anything else?" I asked, jumping in to work.

I didn't stop for hours. People just kept coming through the door and I kept running, pouring glass after glass. Beers and wines and more beers, and the occasional cocktail for a stray Hen Party reveler foolish enough to come to the bar on a football night.

You could barely hear yourself think above the roar of the men in the bar. As I predicted, it was roasting in here; I snagged my water bottle out from under the counter, and gulped it down before wiping the sweat from my brow.

"Who's winning?" I called out at one point to Tammy, grabbing her elbow as she flew past me.

She rolled her eyes and laughed. "You can't tell?"

I winked at her, grinning, and let her disappear back into the crowd.

She knew I wasn't a football girl by any stretch, but living in Nebraska meant you *had* to follow a team—and know the rules well enough to follow along.

"Hey gorgeous. Aren't you dressed like an angel tonight?" said a man leaning over the bar, his tone sticky enough to trap plenty of honey suckers.

But that wasn't me.

I squashed the desire to roll my eyes at his cheesy pick-up line. That would have been strictly against Mick's "no upsetting the customers" policy. Instead, I flashed the guy a grin. "Thanks. I got this top on sale, actually."

I tugged at the top in question. It showed off my ample cleavage, true. But it was made of a breathable cotton, perfect for running around like a crazy woman for eight hours straight, and serving beers to guys like this one. "What can I get you?"

"What are you doing after work tonight?" he pressed on, ignoring my polite deflection.

The smile I'd stuck on my face threatened to slide off. I forced it to stay put.

This guy wasn't a regular. I'd never seen him before. Which was a pity, really. If he *had* been a regular, he would have known that I don't date.

Barely, at any rate.

And even if I did, I wouldn't choose a forty-something guy who wore a suit to a bar on a Saturday night. Who was he trying to impress?

If it had been a Friday, that would've been forgivable. I understood the whole corporate vibe then; some of the men came straight from work, after all, so they had an excuse to be suited up. But this douchebag had actually made the decision to put on a suit to come drink beer and watch football.

"Um... what am I doing after work?" I struggled to think of something brief and innocuous in response. "Probably going home and face-planting my bed. I don't get off until four a.m."

His eyes lit up and this time, I couldn't disguise my flinch.

Fuck! Rookie mistake. Dammit.

I'd gotten out of practice, apparently.

"Well, I'm sure I can get you off by four-thirty." His tongue darted out and wet his lips. "My place or yours?"

My skin crawled. Jeez, this guy.

I can't say I wasn't used to it. Practically everyone in the place had tried it on at least once. After five years working as a bartender, I'd accepted that this sort of thing came with the territory.

Most accepted when I said no.

If only they knew I could shift into a wolf and bite their faces off if I wanted to...

I didn't know if it was the heat, or the lateness of the hour, but something about this dude made me want to punch him right in his smug expression.

I put up my hands and shrugged. "Look, I'm just here to serve drinks. Do you want something?"

"Uh, yeah. Three beers and your phone number."

I turned away to grab three beers from the fridge, the expensive ones. He hadn't been specific, after all. His mistake.

"Are these all right?"

His eyes widened a little as I set the bottles on the counter between us.

"Oh, sorry. Too rich for your blood?" I asked, trying to sound as confused and innocent as possible.

"Oh, no, not at all. Here, charge it." He handed me a normal blue credit card and I bit my tongue.

What? No black AMEX?

I tapped his card on the machine with a bland smile and slid over to the other end of the bar, trying to calm the tremble of anger rushing through my veins.

You can't hit anything, or anyone, here. Relax.

That guy had actually managed to make my blood boil. I wasn't sure why. I was usually pretty good at brushing past people's shit.

Damn, my blood really was up tonight. Definitely must have been the heat. I needed some peppermint tea and about fourteen hours of sleep to calm down. In that order.

"Hi, what can I get you?" I asked the girl waiting patiently for my attention. She was a tiny redhead, fresh out of college by the looks of her.

"Um, white wine please. Just the house is okay."

I nodded at her with a friendly smile, then turned to open the wine cooler.

College and wine. Luxuries I hadn't been able to afford at her age.

Whatever, I'm doing fine without either.

"Here you go." I slid the drink across the bar.

I was just turning to deal with the guy to her left, when an almighty crash reverberated across the room.

The crowd of rowdy patrons stumbled out of the way to reveal the same douchebag who'd been trying to pick me up earlier.

He'd dropped all three bottles of beer against the hardwood floor. There were shards of glass everywhere, and alcohol pooled at his feet.

Shit.

I glanced around, trying to spot Mick. He was all the way over on the other side of the room, busy with the DJ and his sound system.

"Allara!" Mick called, gesturing to the mess on the floor and miming a dustpan and brush. He gave me a thumbs up before turning away again.

I was officially done with this night. I just wanted to go home to bed.

Fine. I picked up a spare tray, grabbed a broom, and headed out into the fray.

The guy was leaning against a nearby pillar, looking strangely smug.

"Hey, I'm sorry," he said, not sounding sorry at all.

I forced a smile. "No problem."

After all, it was my job to clean up after man-babies like him. I bent down and picked up the big pieces of glass carefully, putting them on the tray, and then swept up as much of the rest as possible, into a pile.

Damn it. The glass had tracked everywhere.

I was going to need the vacuum.

I grabbed the tray and turned to the creep. "Can you keep other customers away from this area? I'll be back with the vacuum in a moment."

"Sure thing," he said, with a shit-eating grin.

I turned to walk away and he slapped me on the ass. Hard.

I bit my tongue as a growl rolled up into my throat.

I swallowed hard. That was unusual. My wolf usually lay mostly dormant inside of me.

I shook myself and kept walking. I located the vacuum at the back of the store room, and allowed myself one single, solitary, *"fuck!"* out loud in the dark, empty space, before I went straight back out there.

That creep didn't scare me. *Hardly.* I'd dealt with much worse.

～

Eventually, the football game ended. Most of the patrons had called it a night and were wandering home or piling into waiting cabs.

All of them, that is, except the creep.

I'd kept an eye on him after the beer incident, but he mostly kept a low profile for the rest of the night. Foolishly, I let my guard down, deciding he wasn't worth the stress. If he wanted to nurse his beer in an empty bar, fine. Not my concern; I'd get to kick him out soon, anyway.

Finally, there were only two customers left. The creep and some guy slumped over in a booth in the back corner.

Almost done.

As I wiped down the counter, I noticed the creep harassing Tammy over by the DJ booth. She'd gone out to collect the empty glasses. He was pressing her up against a pillar, tugging at the tray in her hands.

Ah, shit.

My heart began to pump faster. Harder.

Tammy was no wilting lily, but she was no wolf-shifter in hiding either.

"Hey, Mick!" I called out, but he was nowhere to be seen. I ducked my head around the kitchen door. "Louise, you seen Mick?"

"Hmm, not for a while." Louise furrowed her brow, stacking plates onto the draining board. "Bathroom, maybe?"

"Do you mind keeping an eye on the bar? Tammy needs help."

Louise narrowed her eyes, understanding my tone. "Sure."

She came out of the kitchen with me as I re-entered the bar area and marched across the floor. The creep had succeeded in tugging the tray out of Tammy's hands and was leering over her, getting right up in her face.

His breath probably smelled horrible.

"Please," Tammy was begging. "Stop!"

She shrank back against the pillar, trying to fend off his groping hands.

My wolf instantly rose, sensing danger to a member of my

adopted family. I reassured her enough that she settled, albeit uneasily.

I can deal with this, I told my wolf. *He's just another creep who needs to go home and sleep off his stupidity.*

"Hey!" I poked him hard in the shoulder. "That's enough, now."

"Piss off." He glared at me, his eyes bleary and bloodshot. He reeked of alcohol. "You had your chance. I'm going home with this one."

Over his shoulder, I caught Tammy's eye. The look of horror on her face had my heart pounding and my wolf racing straight back up to the surface.

No fucking way.

"I don't think so." I grabbed his arm and yanked him away, giving Tammy the chance to scuttle to safety. "I'm calling you a cab. C'mon, let's go."

I did a quick scan of the room. Damn it, where'd Mick go? Patrick, our security guard, was missing too. He was probably outside making sure the drunk patrons got into cabs instead of wandering toward their parked cars.

"You little bitch!"

My attention snapped back to the problem at hand. The hammered, infuriating *asshole* of a problem standing in front of me with an irate expression.

"You let her get away."

"Get *away?*" My jaw dropped. "She's not a fucking rabbit, dude. You're not out hunting."

The veins on his neck bulged as he clenched his teeth. He wanted to hit me. *Well... good. Just try it! Please. Give me an excuse to break your teeth.*

I held my ground. "I suggest you leave, now, before I call the police."

I turned away, but didn't get very far. Wide hands reached out and grabbed me, hauling me backwards. I could feel his soft belly pressing against my back. His beer breath brushed my cheek.

"You jealous, girly? That your problem?"

I tried to lean away from him, but he held on tight. I felt a hot wetness sliding over my cheek, slithering behind my ear.

Ugh. He had his *tongue* on my *face*.

That, right there, was the last straw.

I shoved away from him as hard as I could and twisted around to face him. He stumbled backwards, a look of shock on his stupid face. Shock that turned almost instantly to rage. As his fists clenched and he started toward me, I roundhouse kicked him in the belly.

He flew backwards and collided with the pillar behind him, clutching his stomach.

"What the fuck?" He wheezed. *Good.* "You're crazy, bitch."

When he stumbled to his feet and staggered forward, his dark eyes were filled with hatred.

His fingers tightened into a fist and he aimed what looked like a forceful haymaker at my head.

Shouldn't signal your punches like that.

I ducked under him and came up with a swift upper cut to his jaw, listening to the satisfying crunch it made as my fist met bone.

Unfortunately, I hadn't put enough force behind the punch. He didn't go down as I'd intended. He just staggered sideways, off kilter, and fumbled for a barstool to hang onto.

"Who the fuck do you think you are?" he hissed. "Stupid bitch."

My strength didn't exactly match that of a normal human woman, especially one my size. He was clearly too drunk to register what I really was.

I grinned; that was his biggest mistake.

He got to his feet and tugged on his suit jacket, stumbling away and weaving through scattered barstools. He mumbled to himself as he went, but I didn't bother to listen closely to what he had to say.

Instead, I moved cautiously back behind the bar, watching his progress. To my relief, he made a beeline for the exit and cursed as he yanked the door open with more force than necessary. Before he could walk out into the night, however, someone stepped in front of him, blocking his path.

We'd dimmed the lights in the bar hours ago, and at first I could only make out the man's silhouette against the darkness.

I could tell that this guy was big, though. Bigger than the creep by a long shot, with a broad chest and shoulders.

It was then that I recognized his flannel shirt. The guy from the booth!

Huh. In the rush to help Tammy, I'd forgotten he was still here.

He wasn't slumped in his booth anymore. He wasn't swaying like the creep, either. On the contrary, he moved with the deliberateness of someone who was completely sober.

He leaned forward, saying something to the creep in a low voice. His face caught the light, and I got a good look at him at last.

God dammit.

"You," I whispered. My heart sped up at the sight of someone I had never thought I'd see again.

Before I could process my thoughts or emotions, the creep swung his fist at the newcomer.

Oh, boy. Even bigger mistake.

The flannel-shirted guy moved so leisurely it almost seemed like slow motion. He hit the creep in the face with one brutal blow, and the douchebag went down like a lead fucking balloon.

REID

It took me more than two weeks to track her down. I'd searched every corner of the city and come up empty. I'd had to rake through social media in my shitty motel room and hang around outside dive bars in the hope someone might have seen her.

And yet, there had been nothing.

Until this morning, when I'd overheard some guys outside a cafe talking about a hot girl they'd seen the other night, a shifter with dark hair who worked weekends at Mick's place.

That had caught my attention, and the lucky break had led me all the way here, to a bar in the middle of the city. I'd been watching

Allara work all night. She really was a sight for sore eyes, even after all this time.

Her gorgeous thick, dark hair swung in a high ponytail as she took orders. Her blue eyes remained warm, no matter who she was dealing with, and her beautiful face glowed with good health. Her strong, lithe arms moved gracefully, gesturing back and forth as she laughed with her customers.

And those were just her physical attributes.

According to my intel, she worked two jobs now. She'd lived alone out here for five years, supporting herself. The fact that she lived outside of the pack's protection was unusual for a shifter woman, even these days. Obviously, she was doing a pretty damn good job of it. She looked well. Not unhappy.

Damn, it was good to see her again.

I stuck to the shadows all night and slouched alone in a booth near the back. I didn't know why, but I was hesitant to catch her attention. Tracking her down had been one thing, but actually confronting her with everything I had to tell her? That was quite another.

So, I lay low and watched her work. She served drinks, took cash, and got hit on. Rinse and repeat. She dealt with all of it in her stride, and better than most.

I knew her well, though. All those little tells from the past, were still in operation. That tiny crease between her eyebrows when she served the guy in the suit, told me she was royally pissed.

And rightly so. That asshole guy just wouldn't let it go. All night I watched him circling the bar like a fly that just couldn't be swatted away.

I managed to keep my cool, even when the other patrons started to leave and the jerk managed to corner Allara's bartender friend. Though, a moment longer and I would have stepped in.

Funnily enough, I hadn't had to.

The fire in Allara's eyes had flared as she'd stormed over and finally confronted the asshole who had been plaguing her all night.

There had been a shadow of her father in her, at that moment. They'd always been cut from the same cloth, with their dark hair and eyes, right down to their hot tempers and their desire to protect others.

When the guy hit the pillar, the thud had reached my booth. I smirked down at the table, hearing her punch meet its mark, right against his stupid face. Atta girl.

Dumb bitch, the guy had muttered to himself as he stumbled away from her. *Probably a whore, anyway.*

I'd heard enough. I wasn't going to let him get away with disrespecting her so easily. I was tired of sitting back and listening to his bullshit. Watching him try to use his strength to abuse and control the women behind the bar.

Time to make my presence known.

Moving swiftly so I could catch him before he disappeared into the night, I blocked his exit, putting my hand against the doorframe so he couldn't slither away.

"What the fuck, man," the guy mumbled. Allara had really done a number on him; with the alcohol and the blows, he could barely stand straight.

I leaned close. "Your pick-up tactics need a little work."

He blinked, his lip curling. "Get fucked…"

He swung at me and that was all the permission I needed.

I punched him. Hard. It was one of the most satisfying punches I've ever landed in my life.

He crumpled to the floor like a sack of potatoes.

I nudged him with my foot, rolling him onto his side. He was out cold. *Huh.* His expensive suit dragged a little, picking up scum from the floor of the bar.

Oops. Hadn't meant to hit him that hard. I kept forgetting humans were more fragile than us.

A wolf would have taken that punch and come back for more.

I swept the hair back off my face and looked up, trying with difficulty to keep my heart rate under control.

Allara, the love of my life, my sweetheart, the one I'd let get away… stood there with her arms crossed, staring at me. I couldn't work out the expression on her face, but I could make a good guess as to what she felt.

Disbelief. Shock. Regret, maybe?

Same as me.

She met my gaze. Her expression cleared, landing firmly on *irritated.*

With her arms folded like that, her boobs looked great. High. Full. Plump. Just like I remembered. I forced my eyes away from that delectable cleavage.

"I had it under control, Reid," she said, forgoing a greeting.

She hasn't changed. Always did cut straight to the chase.

"I know." I grinned at her. "But he deserved it."

We stood there for a moment. Seeing her again, *talking* to her, I was struggling to remember why I'd come here in the first place.

"Uh…" I shifted my weight, glancing around the empty bar. "Can we talk?"

Her arms relaxed and fell to her sides. She rolled her shoulders a little, like she was preparing for battle. "Do I have a choice?"

Always, I wanted to say.

And she did. She could walk away from me right now, disappear again like she had five years ago.

She'd abandoned the pack, her father, all her responsibilities as the Alpha's daughter.

She left me. Even though she'd had good reason to.

I shook the thought away. This was bigger than what had happened in our past; bigger than us. She needed to know what had been going on with the pack since she'd left.

Her pack. *Our* pack.

We needed her now. She was the only thing that stood between us and Jaime.

"You know you have a choice," I said, keeping my voice low and persuasive. "But if you have a minute, I'd appreciate it."

She stared at me, assessing me intently like she used to. And for one unsettling moment, I thought she was going to turn away, tell me to *fuck off* and leave her alone. The thought made me cold.

Then her shoulders relaxed a little, and I realized we'd both been holding our breaths. She nodded once.

"Fine," she said. "I finish in an hour, okay? I can talk to you then. Or tomorrow. It's super late."

I couldn't wait any longer to speak to her. I'd been waiting all night. Longer than that, really. Five whole years.

I wasn't tired. Far from it. Watching her all night, talking with her now, standing up close like this... it was enough to call the wolf in me up to the surface.

I could feel the pheromones shivering through my body, urging me to shift.

But I had to ignore the way my blood was pumping in her presence.

Ignore the enticing scent that filled my nostrils every time she moved.

Mate.

But she wasn't. She had made that choice when she ran.

Which meant, I couldn't act on those urges now, no matter how strong they were.

My desire for her was forbidden.

Sadly, I answered to a higher power than my libido.

With difficulty, I shoved down the distracting feelings and refocused. I had a job to do, after all.

"I can wait." I looked around and pointed to an empty booth. "Can we chat there?"

She wrinkled her nose. "I've been here all night. There's a twenty-four-hour diner just down the block. I'll meet you there, okay?"

"Sure."

Allara turned away, heading back to the bar and picking up a tray.

Conversation closed, then.

It was about what I deserved, anyway.

I stared down at the unconscious guy at my feet, half wondering if I should drag him outside.

A bouncer appeared through the open door behind me and tsked at the sight of him, shaking his head. "Friend of yours?"

I snorted. "Hardly."

With one final, wistful glance toward Allara, I made my way out the door, leaving the creep and his future fate in the hands of the bouncer.

He must have caught something in my expression, because he clapped me on the shoulder as I passed and hooked a thumb toward the bar. Allara had busied herself with the cash register: she'd apparently decided to ignore my presence completely.

"You know Allara, then?" the bouncer asked.

"I..." I opened my mouth and shut it again.

He waited.

"Used to," I mumbled eventually, ducking my head at the sight of the guy's knowing grin and raised brow. He was clearly looking out for her, but must have known her well enough not to try stepping in on her behalf.

As I strode out into the night, it began to dawn on me. This mission was going to be a whole lot more difficult than I'd realized.

Allara had a life here, one that I didn't know anything about. Friends. Maybe even a boyfriend. The latter thought turned my stomach.

After all my efforts, finding her again had turned out to be the easy part.

Convincing her to give up her life here in the city? That was going to be a whole other level of difficult

CHAPTER 3
ALLARA

Reid was the last person in the world I expected to see tonight.

The last person I wanted to see—tonight, or any night, for that matter.

He was the guy—the *only* guy—who had completely broken my heart.

He'd always gotten to me like no-one else, even when we were kids. He understood me in ways I didn't understand myself. And then, one day, he ripped it all away like what we had was nothing.

He was one who got away. Only, it ended up being me that got away. From him, and from everything I had known and grown up with.

As I started packing away glasses, my memories burst through, creating a kaleidoscope of images flashing past me, one after another.

The day I first saw him. We'd been kids then, total strangers. Too young to shift, chasing each other through the trees with sticks and howling like wildcats all summer long, running barefoot over the forest floor.

The picture changed. The two of us in awkward adolescence, struggling to cope with the rush of puberty and our first shift. Reid had withdrawn, avoided me for weeks, disturbed by the new, hormone-fueled feelings that were racing through him.

Then, later, Reid and I in bed together. Our first time together.

My first time... period.

He'd been so gentle, letting me set the pace. I recalled his broad shoulders beneath my fingertips, warm and strong, the silken feel of his hair that always seemed to fall down into his eyes no matter what he did to it. The shape of his mouth, curled up at one corner, right before he kissed me. All the tiny details were still there in my mind as I recalled the memory of that night.

As the years wore on, our connection had only deepened. Couples around us broke up and got back together, found new partners who came and went as the seasons changed.

But not us. Our teenage infatuation morphed into a true, lasting bond. I'd been crazy for him. He was everything I thought a good man should be: strong, warm, funny. He was a part of my pack.

A part of *me*.

I would have done anything for him, and back then I had truly believed he do anything for me in return.

That hope had been snuffed out the night Reid broke up with me.

He had acted so strange that night; distracted. All he would say was that it wasn't right for us to be together. That he knew it was hard, but that one day I'd understand.

I'm doing this for you, he said. *Because I care about you.*

He hadn't given me a reason beyond that. Instead, he'd just stood there, stone faced, while I yelled at him, crying, and begged him to change his mind.

I couldn't remember most of what I'd said after that. I only knew that I could never take any of it back.

I'd packed some things in a small suitcase and left the following morning.

I watched everything I'd ever known shrinking away from the back window of the cab as it drove through the trees.

My pack, my people, my friends, my family.

And now, here he was. The person from my old life I'd fought hardest to forget.

There was only one reason he'd track me down after all this time, and I knew it had nothing to do with him missing an old flame.

Something must be wrong with the pack.

Or my dad.

That was the only reason I hadn't immediately told him to leave.

I finished up my shift by putting away the final glass and glancing around to make sure there was nothing left to do. I walked up to my boss who was counting the money out of the till, and handed my apron back with a grimace.

"You gotta get more security staff. We could have been in a hell of a lot of trouble tonight if I hadn't kicked that guy's ass."

Mick grinned at me as he took the apron. A girl waited for him at other end of the bar, gazing in his direction with big doe eyes.

So *that* was where he'd been all night.

"That's why I have you, kiddo." He ruffled my hair and I ducked away from him.

He chuckled. "You're all the security I need."

"You know I do the work of two bartenders, right?" I stuck out my tongue at him. "You can't count on me for security too. That's just not fair."

"Hey." As he handed me my pay, he pulled an extra fifty from the till and pressed it into my hand with a wink. "Thanks for tonight, hon."

Tammy wandered out from the kitchen, wrapped up in her woolen sweater and hugging herself tightly. The ordeal had clearly shaken her. "Yeah, Allara. I owe you one."

That was my problem, I thought with a sigh. My famous protective streak.

I couldn't walk away from people who needed me, and everyone knew it.

Even people who had crushed my heart under their heel for no good reason, then turned up five years later as if nothing had happened.

Damn it.

I tried to tamp down my pulse rate, which surged at the thought of Reid waiting in the diner down the road.

"I'll see you both tomorrow night, okay?" I managed a smile at Tammy and Mick, and raised my hand in farewell.

Hopefully, Sunday night would be quieter, and far less eventful.

Pulling on my long woolen coat, I shook my hair free from its ponytail and walked out into the crisp night air.

I smelled Reid immediately. The intensity of his wolf shifter pheromones mingled with his cologne and an underlying scent that definitely hadn't changed in the five years since I'd seen him. The evocative smell melted the years away and I had to stifle the moan that rose up from my chest.

I would never get enough of that scent. I would never forget it, either.

"I thought I'd walk with you," he said, the voice coming out of the darkness.

I startled, then looked to the right where he was leaning against a brick wall, his head cocked at a sexy angle like some sort of underwear model about to strip off.

"Okay." I shrugged, like it didn't matter either way, though my heart was thudding through my winter layers. "No problem."

I stuck my hands into the pockets of my coat and began to walk.

I loved how dark the nights became at this time of year. The cold kept the city streets quiet and deserted, but there was still enough light from the stars shining brightly above us to see clearly enough to navigate.

It was a pity we were surrounded by so many streetlights here. Without them, we'd be able to appreciate a lot more of the natural light.

Still, this time of night, after my shifts, was the closest my concrete jungle came to the vast, glittering constellations I'd been used to seeing, growing up.

Reid and I had gazed up at those same constellations once. We had given them made-up names, and I picked out all the brightest stars, pointing them out one by one.

"I'll make them into a necklace, Allie. Just for you."

"Reid!" I'd giggled. "You can't make stars into necklaces."

"I can." He kissed the top of my head. "For you, I can. I promise."

When I glanced in his direction, his head was tilted up toward the heavens.

He glanced over, and our eyes met. Was he remembering those times, too?

It felt like a lifetime ago.

The diner was up ahead, just around the corner. We kept walking in silence.

Was he as weirded out by all of this as I was?

I couldn't think of anything useful to say. I had a million questions rolling around in my head, but my mind turned blank every time I tried to reach for one.

His presence alone was intoxicating. We walked close enough that I could feel the radiant heat from his body, and our hands were inches away from each other as we reached the end of the block.

I tried to tell myself that it didn't matter how sexy he was, or how much heat he put out, inviting my hands to touch and explore. Reid, and everything I had ever loved about him, was in my past. And that's where he needed to stay.

My body wasn't listening.

Heat pooled in my lower belly, and my skin tingled. My heart thumped and blood pounded in my ears.

"It's..." I began, then fumbled when he caught my eye. "Uh. It's right here."

The bell jangled when I opened the door.

He inclined his head, indicating that I should go first. "After you."

A reluctant smile twisted my lips.

What could I say? The guy was a gentleman. He was exactly as I remembered him, and I knew we'd be standing here all night while he pushed to do the right thing.

He always had.

Which was why our breakup had felt like such a betrayal.

The thought pulled at my stomach, and my smile faded as I walked into the diner.

"Hey, Penny," I called out to the waitress standing behind the cash register. "Got room for two more?"

I'd known Penny for five years, ever since I started working for Mick. She was tough, like me, and she'd helped me out of some tight corners when I first arrived in the city.

"Allara, hi!" Penny's gaze darted around the empty diner, and she chuckled. "Yeah, I think we can squeeze you in."

I started toward my favorite booth at the front of the shop.

She raised an eyebrow, as if noticing Reid for the first time and liking what she saw.

Her eyes widened, and her brows waggled at me. "Want some menus? Maybe a candle?"

I gave her a frown, trying to quash where her thoughts were obviously headed. "Menu, yes," I said, sliding into the booth. "Candle, definitely not."

Reid sat down opposite me and drummed his hands against the table. "You come here a lot?"

"Yeah, it's kind of the only decent place open after I finish work," I said. "I'm usually wired and starving, so I need someplace to relax before I head home."

After not being able to speak at all, now I was talking too much, too fast. Trying to fill the empty space between us with words.

His presence in the city felt like a bizarre fever dream, my old life crashing gracelessly into my new one. Part of me worried that if I blinked, he might melt away.

"Night shift munchies." Reid nodded. "Makes sense."

Huh.

For us, it didn't make sense at all.

The wolf shifters of my old pack weren't nocturnal creatures at all. They hunted, fought, and conducted their business in the daylight hours.

Up with the sun, down with the sun, as my daddy always said.

Reid must have been feeling pretty shitty having to stay up so late to talk to me. Maybe that was the reason he was acting so oddly. He hadn't met my gaze once since we'd sat down.

"You want some coffee?" I asked.

"No, thanks," he said. "I'll be bouncing off the walls 'til dawn if I have some now."

Penny came up to our booth with the menus. She looked Reid up and down like she'd never seen a man before. Or at least, not one that good-looking. She turned to me and mouthed, *who is he?*

Later, I mouthed back, hiding my face behind my menu. Reid was paying us no attention, however; he was fixated on his order.

She shrugged, but her eyes glinted with interest, nevertheless. "The usual, Allara?"

I couldn't blame her for being curious. Reid didn't exactly blend in with the city suits. I'd never even seen him wear a tie. His flannel shirt and beat up leather jacket made him stick out around here, and his height and broad physique only accentuated his striking looks.

It wasn't my style to bring random men to my favorite diner at the end of my shift, and Penny knew it. I would have to give her a rundown later.

That'll be an interesting conversation.

I nodded. "Yes, please."

Blackberry tea and a piece of pecan pie. My reward at the end of a long, exhausting night.

Predictably, Reid ordered half the menu. I laughed at him when Penny walked away and propped my chin in my hands, resting my elbows on the table.

"Still hungry as ever, huh?"

"My appetite hasn't changed, if that's what you mean," he said slowly.

I swallowed hard and stared into his dark eyes.

Did that mean that he still liked to have sex every day and twice on Sundays?

Because that was an appetite I could appreciate.

I coughed, crossing my legs under the table and dropping my gaze quickly.

Jeez. I needed to shut down that line of thinking, and quickly.

Whatever sex drive I once possessed had lain dormant for a long time. One whiff of Reid's scent, however, and I couldn't seem to get my mind out of the gutter.

"You wanted to talk." I drew a deep breath, forcing myself to look at him and praying that the heat I could feel in my face wasn't a noticeable blush. "So, start talking."

A shadow fell over Reid's face, and he stared through the window at the darkness outside.

It was bad news, then, just as I had suspected.

My heart sank and I clutched my hands together.

"Your father's sick."

My stomach swooped. "How sick?"

Alpha wolves were the strongest of our kind, and pack leaders were the toughest of all. They rarely got ill, but if they did, it usually signaled the end of an era.

Reid lowered his head, staring at me with an intensity that I remembered well.

"You know what I mean, Allara."

I shook my head. Pain tightened my ribcage until I felt like my chest would burst. "I need you to say it."

"He's dying," Reid said, sounding shaky. "The doctors haven't said how long he has left, but... you and I both know they don't understand our physiology very well."

"But..." I scrambled for words as I tried to process the information. I'd expected bad news, and yet somehow, not this. "Are we talking—what? Weeks, months... years?"

I knew in my heart that Reid wouldn't be here if it was the latter.

"Weeks. At most."

Hot tears sprang up in my eyes and I ducked my head and blinked rapidly, forcing them back. I refused to cry, not here, and not in front of Reid.

"What..." I swiped at my cheek, catching a stray tear. *Damn it.* "What can I do?"

My dad and I hadn't been close, even when I lived with the pack. Not after my mother had died, anyway. It happened suddenly, the year I turned fourteen. Dad withdrew from almost everyone, shutting himself away in his study for months and taking long, solitary walks around the perimeter of the village.

Eventually he'd begun to open up again, but we had never really re-connected like we had in the past. As the years wore on, I had turned to Reid rather than Dad for comfort.

But he was still my dad, and to hear now, that he had mere weeks...

The night I'd left the pack, the look on my father's face was etched onto my memory.

He had stood watching me, like an unmoving stone statue. He didn't say anything. He didn't need to.

"You have to come back, Allara," Reid whispered, breaking me out of my thoughts. "You have to come back with me."

"I…" I frowned, trying to think. "I'll come back, sure. To see Dad. I won't be staying, though."

Reid matched my frown with his own. "You know that's not what I meant, Allara."

"Well, what *did* you mean? Be clear."

Something contrary inside made me want to push at him until he acknowledged the unspoken threat of his presence to my current, comfortable existence.

He glared at me, and I glared back, my sadness temporarily forgotten.

That was the problem with us, the thing everyone had loved to point out in the past. We had been a hot-headed pair. I needed someone calm, like a chilled-out yoga instructor. A guy who could balance me out, and temper the fire in my blood.

"The pack is waiting for you, Allara. It is time to claim your birthright."

I stared at him, dumbfounded.

I hadn't expected *that*.

"I…" I struggled to form a coherent thought. *This cannot be happening.* "You… What are you *talking* about? Dad's been grooming Jaime to take over for…ever!"

Jaime was the son of Terry, my dad's right-hand man. He was a beta like his father, but fierce with ambition. I'd never really gotten on with him, but I'd always chalked it up to my own jealousy; he and my dad had been super close.

Especially after Mom died.

Jaime had become the son my father never had: strong, sharp, and most importantly, *male*. I found it difficult to watch them together, so I'd kept my distance from Jaime out of habit.

I thought back to that time. About a week before Reid broke my heart, Dad had gathered the whole pack together for a huge feast. He'd pulled Jaime up to stand by his side, his arm thrown affectionately around Jaime's shoulders as he made a toast.

He declared then and there that, when the time came for the pack to have a new Alpha, Jaime would be his successor.

I hadn't been surprised. None of us were. That announcement had been years in the making.

I'd never really thought about the timing of it all, though. Jaime was announced as my dad's heir, and Reid ended our relationship a few days later.

In hindsight, that struck me as kind of odd.

Nevertheless, what was done, was done. I'd tried my best to close the book on that chapter of my life for a reason. Re-examining those memories was like poking at an old wound. It wouldn't bring me the closure I wanted.

It would only reignite the pain.

"I know it's not what you want to hear." He looked down at the table top for a moment.

Damn it. It was all I could do not to reach out and comb my fingers through his hair, tilt his face up to mine, and press a kiss onto his lips.

Oh, how I had missed kissing Reid.

I blinked, bringing my focus back to the matter at hand as Reid spoke.

"It's not meant to be this way, Allara. *You* are your father's heir. His *blood*."

I shrugged off his words, along with my traitorous impulses.

"This is what my dad wanted. Your Alpha. He chose Jaime." I narrowed my eyes. "Then you dumped me, remember? There was nothing left. So, yeah, I got out."

Now it seemed to be my turn to stare down at the wood grain of the table. Anger filled my chest as I raised my gaze back up. "Has anything changed? No, of course it hasn't."

Reid went very still, like he'd been caught in a trap he hadn't realized was there.

"Allara..." He lifted his head and glowered at me.

Like *he* had any right to be angry.

"Jaime isn't the man your father thinks he is. He can't be trusted. And there's no one who can stand up to him worth a damn, not anymore." He leaned forward, capturing my gaze. "No one but you."

His eyes were hypnotic. For one heart-fluttering moment I felt like I would do anything he asked, even dive off a cliff top if he suggested it.

A plate of pie landed heavily in front of me, followed by a steaming mug of tea. I snapped out of my love-struck spell and thanked Penny with a flustered smile. Her answering grin was a little too knowing for my liking.

With my first sip of tea, my faculties returned. Was Reid being *serious* right now?

"I'm sorry to have to tell you this," I said, not sorry in the slightest, "but your trip has been wasted. Eat up, get your strength back, and go home. There's no way I'm going back with you. Not now." *Not unless Dad's really that sick...*

He had the gall to look confused. "Why not?"

I'd been about to take my first bite of pie. Instead, I dropped my fork and it fell against the side of the plate with a clatter.

"Why *not?* I have a life here, in case you haven't noticed. Friends, an apartment. I have work tomorrow, for Christ's sake! And I'm not giving it up, Reid. Any of it. If Dad's that unwell, then I'll make arrangements to come visit. But not to stay. Never that." I picked up my fork again and pointed it at him. "Not for anyone."

"But—"

My words rushed out before I could stop them, buoyed by a tidal wave of past heartbreak and loss. "And *certainly* not for you."

CHAPTER 4
REID

I gazed at Allara. This booth wasn't huge, and she was sitting close enough to touch.

My first love. Hell, my *only* love.

No matter how hard I'd tried to put her out of my mind, I always failed. She'd made a permanent mark on my heart; one I would carry forever.

"Allara." Somehow, I had to make her understand. "This is serious. The whole pack is in jeopardy—every last man, woman and child."

She would come around eventually. I was sure of it.

The Allara I remember was fiercely protective. She cared deeply for her pack and defended them no matter what kind of trouble they got into. She might be tough, but she was also a good person who cared about others. Her heart had always been in the right place. I couldn't see that changing, no matter what she'd been through in the past five years.

The way she'd punched that guy in the face for her friend tonight? That was Allara all over.

Now, she just stared at me with those beautiful dark eyes, and pushed my plate closer toward me. "Eat up, okay? You have a long drive ahead of you."

I stifled a sigh. So, maybe convincing Allara to come back with me wasn't going to be as easy a task as I thought, but I couldn't really blame her.

Her father had distanced himself from her after her mother died —a time when she probably needed her dad more than ever. Then he had passed her over as his successor, and on top of that, I'd gone and ended our relationship. Five years ago, every link she had to the pack must have felt like they had been broken, one by one. She must have felt abandoned by everyone.

I hung my head. There wasn't any point ruminating on the past. I had to focus on the situation in front of me, and consider the future.

I picked up my knife and fork and began to eat. The scrambled eggs were light and fluffy, the bacon crunchy and fatty. Just how I liked it. Focusing on the food gave me time to gather my thoughts and figure out how best to play this.

Allara matched my silence, though I noticed she only picked sporadically at her pie. No matter what she said, I could tell my news had upset her.

She hadn't changed much. Still beautiful, stubborn, and fiery. Everything I remembered. Everything I loved.

If I moved my leg under the table, even slightly, it would brush against her calf. The prospect was enticing, but there was something in her eyes that made me hesitate.

Her eyes *had* changed. They used to glow when she looked at me, lighting up her whole face with a radiance that took my breath away.

I hadn't been naïve enough to expect to find the lovestruck teenager I'd once known. I knew that time was over, and that she had buried her teenage notions when she left all those years ago.

But I hadn't expected the loss of innocent young love to sting this much. She was so close to me, but her face was pale and blank. Her cold demeanor separated us, far more than this table; it made me feel like the miles still stretched out between us.

I didn't know how to get through to her. I didn't know if I *could*.

Suddenly, the Allara I'd known seemed like a figment of imagination I'd dreamt up, a ghost from a happier time. One that was not even real.

Once I'd eaten the breakfast plate and the French toast, my hunger began to abate. I moved on to the basket of fries, eating them slowly and stirring my milkshake.

Time to try a different angle, I guess.

"So..." I leaned my elbow on the table. "Tell me about city life then. Since you love it so much. What's so great about it?"

She smiled tightly, but the show of humor didn't reach her eyes.

"I *do* love it." She drew a shaky breath. "I work at an elementary school during the week, helping children with reading issues. And I work weekends at Mick's bar. I've got a lot of friends out here. Good people. They really, uh, helped me through stuff."

I nodded, ignoring the twinge of guilt in my chest.

Did they help her through what I did to her?

"You live alone?"

Do you have a boyfriend? I desperately wanted to know. I sensed the question wouldn't be a welcome one, though.

"Yeah, I do." She looked down at her empty mug, hair hanging over her face.

With a jolt, I thought for a second she had confessed to having a *boyfriend*. I picked up the thread of our conversation as she continued and shook myself internally.

Stay on track, damn it.

Her presence was getting to me, just like it always had. When Allara was near, my brain still turned to mush.

"To be honest, I really like having a place to myself," she said. "You know what growing up in the pack is like. Everyone's living on top of one another, and everyone knows everybody's business. I have my own space here, independence. The city... you can blend in here. Disappear. No one cares what you're doing. I like that anonymity. It's refreshing."

You can disappear? How could someone like Allara disappear? She had such a presence about her. She lit up every room she entered.

Still, I could see why the city held its charms for her. If she hadn't felt welcome at home, the close-knit pack atmosphere would have only magnified the problem. She must have felt trapped.

Especially after... that night.

"You don't love me anymore?"

Something broke inside me at the forlorn note in her voice, but I kept my gaze stoic and controlled.

"I've made up my mind, Allara."

Shoving down the past with some effort, I managed to catch her eye once more.

"Allara. You gotta come home, okay? Even... even if it's just to spend some time with your dad."

Her lovely face crumpled. I hated having to be the one to hurt her —again, but it had to be said. Her father was dying.

"I have some leave due." She sighed, fiddling with her fork. "I'll apply for some in the next few weeks."

What? No!

"That might be too late," I snapped.

Her face blanked, then her eyes narrowed as she glared at me. "Dad hasn't contacted me in five years, Reid. *Five years.* Not once since I left. He never even checked to see if his own daughter was still alive! Do you know how that feels? Why would I just drop everything

I've built here in the city to go running back to a family that so clearly doesn't want me?"

The words were harsh, but I heard the underlying hurt beneath them.

The waitress glanced over at us from behind the counter, looking concerned. I exhaled with frustration and forced myself to lower my voice.

"He does want you, Allara. He's always wanted you." I resisted the urge to reach across the table and grab her hand. "That's not what this is about."

She made a succession of angry noises as she stood, throwing some money down on the table.

I shook my head. I knew she was upset, but *seriously?* She was leaving, just like that?

"Well, thanks for stopping by." She shoved her bag onto her shoulder. "Drive safe. Send my regards to the pack."

As she made to walk past me, my hand shot out and I grabbed her wrist. She tried to shrug me off, but I held tight.

"Reid." She fixed me with an icy gaze. "Let me go."

I could feel her anger rising, and the spark lit the flame to my own temper.

Allara had always done strange things to my insides. As much as we riled each other up, I never felt more alive than when I was with her.

As uncomfortable as this interaction had been, I couldn't deny it: just *being* with her again was exhilarating. I felt more energy sparking through my system than I'd had in years.

"I won't give up that easily, Allara," I assured her. "This is more important than you think."

She twisted sharply and pulled free of my grasp. "Goodnight, Reid."

As she stormed out of the diner, she let the door slam on her way out. I deliberately turned back to my meal rather than see her leave.

I'd already watched her run out of my life once before, and it had been one of the hardest things I'd ever done.

I finished my meal in silence, ignoring the waitress's glower, before heading back to the motel where I'd been staying for the past few nights.

I wasn't leaving this city without Allara. I just had to make her an offer she couldn't refuse.

~

I was so fatigued I practically passed out back in the motel room. I stayed that way all day, trying to catch up on the sleep I'd lost last night. It had been hell trying to adapt my body to the stupid hours these city people keep on weekends. The pack didn't live like this; we went to bed at night rather than dawn. Here, waking up as night fell left me groggy and disoriented.

I couldn't wait to leave this place.

If everything played out as I hoped it would, I would be going home in a few hours.

I just needed to convince Allara that it was a good idea for her to come with me.

I glanced around the parking lot and stared at the small bar. Mick's place, she'd called it, with a note of affection in her voice.

Sunday night seemed to be a quieter affair; only a handful of punters passed through the frosted glass doors, and the noise level was thankfully reduced to a muted hum.

The city could be so loud.

I didn't know how she'd stuck it out for so long.

After a moment of consideration, I decided not to try my luck inside tonight, instead waiting out on the street. I was relieved when she walked out around midnight.

"Hey," I called out, waving at her.

She froze. Her eyes met mine with a mixture of anger and incredulity.

I stayed where I was, leaning against the hood of my truck, letting her assess my presence.

Never catch an unknown shifter off guard, Reid.

But Allara wasn't unknown. I knew the sound of her heartbeat as well as I knew my own.

We'd had sex in this truck I was leaning against... how many times?

God only knows.

I wasn't scrapping the thing, ever. Too many memories I couldn't let go of.

The ghost of a smile flitted across her face as her eyes traced over the scratched headlights and beat-up hubcaps.

"Still got this old junker, then."

"Yep."

I left it at that. There were too many thorns attached to any conversation about our old relationship, and I'd already proven myself adept at stumbling right into them, and scratching both of us in the process.

She cocked her head to the side as she gazed at me. "What are you still doing here, Reid? I told you to go home."

Hopefully my gamble would pay off. After all, the Alpha's daughter had never backed down from a challenge before.

Ever.

"I've got a proposition for you."

Her head came up. I watched her spine straighten into a posture I recognized.

"Oh yeah? What's that?" she asked, lifting her chin.

"A challenge."

Something flickered behind her eyes.

I continued. "A fight, between you and me."

"A fight?" she whispered.

The shifter swirl of silver swam in her eyes.

Wolf shifter eyes. She could try to hide it all she liked from her precious city friends, but she couldn't hide her shifter from me.

"Yeah. If I can pin you, then you gotta come back with me." I lowered my voice and leaned close. "Come see your dad. Come back home, to your pack. Your family. We need you, Allara."

She blinked, seemingly caught off guard, before appearing to recover herself.

"And when *you* lose?" she asked, flicking her ponytail over her shoulder and thrusting out her perky breasts in a cocky move.

I put up my hands, trying to appear as non-threatening as possible.

She'd always been easy to rile up, just like I was. But I sensed that it had been a long time since the wolf in her had been allowed to roam free.

That'll sure make my job easier.

I brushed off my guilt and focused on my task. I had to do whatever it took to get Allara to come back with me, even if that meant using her wolf shifter biology against her.

I gave a loose shrug. "Then I go on my way. I'll return to the pack, admit defeat, and make sure none of us ever bother you again."

I studied her carefully, wondering what she was thinking. If I lost, did she even plan to come home for her father's funeral?

My resolve firmed. It didn't matter what she planned or didn't plan. I was going to win this fight. I had to. I didn't have time to give even a passing thought to the possibility of failure.

She stared at me for a moment longer, and a spark of hope grew in my chest.

Then, she shook her head. "No."

She turned away and walked off without another word.

God dammit.

I took off after her down the street. It looked like she was heading toward that diner where we'd eaten last night.

"Come on, Allara. You know I don't give up that easily."

She stopped in her tracks and pinned me with a stare. "You gave up on *us*."

I felt her words slide like a knife right between my ribs.

"I didn't give up," I forced myself to say. "I made a choice."

She held my gaze for a long time, but I didn't break the eye contact. I couldn't. This was too important.

Eventually, she was the one who blinked and glanced away.

"Then it was the wrong choice." Her voice shook with suppressed emotion.

This time, her words twisted themselves straight into my heart.

I had given her five years to move on, to find someone better, but from everything I'd seen and heard about her time in the city, it didn't seem like she had come close to settling down with anyone else.

I grabbed her arm and pulled her around to face me.

"We need to put our differences aside. It's like I said, okay? There's more at stake here than just the two of us." I understood her position. It was a struggle to think about the bigger picture right now, too. "Accept my challenge, Allara. Let the chips fall where they may."

She bit her lip, and I could tell she was wavering. I gripped her arm a little tighter, pressing my advantage.

"You could be free of me forever. Free of the pack. One fight, that's all it would take. I give you my word. If I lose, I leave."

She lifted her gaze to me, and there was so much unsaid in those big blue eyes of hers. Fear was at the forefront.

Was she afraid of saying no, or saying yes?

Of finally severing her connection to the only true family she had? Our pack.

I hoped not. That was what I had leveraged my challenge on.

Then suddenly her face cleared. She gave a single nod.

"Okay Reid." She cleared her throat, her wide mouth narrowing to a thin line. "I accept your challenge."

Finally.

I knew, somewhere underneath that slick city demeanor, that the Allara I knew was still there.

I shoved my hands into my pockets and projected an aura of

casual certainty. Not that I was feeling anything near casual, but I didn't want my eagerness to cause her to switch off again.

"Where do you want to do this?" I asked, resisting the urge to say, *your place or mine?*

This is her territory, after all.

She knew the lay of the land better than I did.

"My condo has a backyard," she said, without hesitation. "The sooner we can get this over with, the better, right?"

I nodded. "Sure."

I couldn't quite get a handle on her emotions. One moment she seemed ready to kick me to the curb and send me packing, and the next, I could swear she seemed almost... *excited* by the prospect of letting out her wolf.

Without another word, she turned and strode away from me.

She's probably just looking forward to body-slamming me a few times.

Feeling strangely like I'd lost control of the situation, I followed her.

CHAPTER 5
ALLARA

The backyard of my condo was dimly lit, and the fences were high enough to deter any prying neighbors.

Perfect.

I shucked off my scarf and shoved it into my bag. "C'mon, I haven't got all night."

I was trying to contain the rush of adrenaline rocketing through my system, but it was proving more difficult than I thought to tamp the runaway emotions back down.

"Yes ma'am." He gave me a mock salute, and I rolled my eyes.

I could hear the thud of his heartbeat in his chest and his

breathing picking up. My stomach tingled with anticipation despite everything. It had been... how many years since I'd shifted?

Too many.

I grinned, despite the situation that had led to this moment.

"A few ground rules," he said, tugging off his jacket and tossing it to one side. "No hair pulling, okay?"

"Very funny," I replied.

"I remember your moves well enough." He shook himself out a little and stretched. His biceps pulled tight behind his head and I looked away.

What was I *doing*, getting into this with Reid? I was here in the city for a reason. I had an okay life. I had friends. I was doing fine on my own. *Good*, even.

No thanks to him, or my dad, or anyone from the pack.

They'd cut me loose, and never followed up. Till now.

He smirked; he'd caught me looking. I shook the hair out of my face and straightened, focused on keeping my balance.

If he wanted a fight, he would get one. I wasn't going down easy.

Something in his gaze shifted when he registered the change in my posture. To a human, the change would be imperceptible, but for the first time that night I saw the wolf inside him rear up.

His breathing had deepened and there was a silver glint in his eye. My body was responding, as it had done hundreds of times before. Adrenaline raced along my veins, making my muscles tremble, and a shot of excitement curved my lips upward.

My wolf pushed, hard, desperate to be let out after all this time.

Silently, Reid extended his hand to me.

I stared at it for a moment before accepting the connection. Already, my brain felt totally scrambled.

Right. Challenge accepted.

I took a deep breath, and let him clasp our palms together. The feeling of his warm skin amidst the cold night air shocked me, and I gasped.

This was the first time we had touched each other in five years.

His head lowered and his eyes darkened, unblinking, hungry, and utterly focused on me.

I couldn't suppress a shiver as I backed up a couple of steps. He matched me pace for pace, and we began to circle each other slowly.

Without warning, he snarled, and his eyes flashed silver.

The outside world melted away, and my vision narrowed.

He had been my sole focus since we set foot in my backyard, but as I shifted into my wolf body, that feeling only grew in intensity. My every sense flooded with him: the heat of his fur, the intoxication of his scent, the flash of his eyes. They all melted together with a level of concentration I had long forgotten.

I shrank away from him, disorientated and overwhelmed.

It was surreal to be a wolf again, after all this time. My ears flicked, catching the sounds of distant traffic on the freeway.

I padded toward Reid with a curious huff, absorbing the feel of the damp grass against my paws.

Well, they always said it would be like riding a bike.

Reid's wolf eyed me impassively. His brown fur glinted with silver flecks, just like I remembered. He stood a couple of hands taller than me, and his pelt wasn't quite as sleek as mine.

He made a formidable sight. If he had been a stranger, I might have been afraid.

But I wasn't. Quite the opposite, in fact.

He was trembling a little, muscles coiled. He was holding himself back as he waited for me to adjust to the change.

I thought about the long years I'd spent alone. Without him.

I'd been abandoned at a time when I needed him, more than I ever had before. He knew how much he'd hurt me, and he hadn't seemed to care.

And then, to come swanning back into my life now, like nothing had ever happened.

The dark thoughts swirled in my head, and a growl built in my throat.

He answered it with a low, rumbling snarl.

There wasn't any warning or signal. We didn't need one. Not when we were like this.

We sprang at each other, just as we had done countless times before.

But this was no play fight or teenage sparring session. Not for me.

I channeled every ounce of hurt I had held onto for the last five years and unleashed it on him.

It had always been like a dance, fighting with Reid. I could sense his every breath, perceive his movements almost before he actioned them himself, and he could sense mine. We knew each other's strengths and weaknesses as well as we knew our own.

We sparred for a while, ducking and weaving and play fighting as we had as children, re-learning each other as my body quickly fell back into the groove of the whole wolf thing.

I might not have been as strong as I once was, but I knew I could still put up a fight. He seemed to sense the heat of my anger, too. *Good.*

But he was holding back a little, and that infuriated me further.

He'd challenged *me*, after all. There was too much at stake for half measures.

I snapped at him to show my frustration.

He loped back a few paces, shaking out his pelt.

He couldn't fool me. We were both panting heavily with exertion, but he needed to commit fully, so I could, too.

I let out an impatient whine and charged him. Taking advantage of his shock at my aggressive move, I fastened my teeth into his neck and pulled him over me, trying to lock him into a tussle.

He threw me off with ease, confirming my suspicions that he wasn't using his full strength.

Come on, Reid. What're you so afraid of?

He'd been the one to suggest this, raising the stakes. But now we were here, body-slamming each other into the turf, he didn't seem to want to land a proper hit on me.

Finally, it dawned on me. He was worried about hurting me.

I snorted.

Well, if he wanted to hold back, I wouldn't. I slid under him, rolling him over and forcing him into action. We grappled, and finally, I felt his energy engage.

Good. If I won this, I wanted it to be on my own merits, not because he wouldn't commit.

Neither one of us managed to gain the upper hand. His body pressed itself against mine, eliciting all kinds of long-forgotten sensations.

He wasn't going easy on me anymore; he was finally exerting his full strength. I had to use every trick I had to keep him from getting close enough to pin me down.

We drew apart and he shook himself out with a rumbling growl, glowering at me. His eyes darkened, and his pupils grew larger so that only a sliver of silver iris was visible.

Adrenaline pulsed through me.

Perhaps he'd thought I'd go down easy. I hadn't been in my wolf form for a long time, after all, and clearly, he had only grown in agility and strength.

I still had a key advantage over him. Alpha blood ran through my veins. We were more evenly matched than he'd bargained for.

His sudden attack caught me off guard, knocking me to the ground. I twisted out from under him and we rolled over and over on the grass before thudding into the side of the fence, hard enough that splinters of wood flew everywhere.

Oops. So much for keeping a low profile.

For a split second, I had him exactly where I wanted him. His head pushed into the ground and he relaxed under me, huffing out a breath.

I breathed out too, relief crashing over me.

I had this.

Acting on instinct, I leaned down and nuzzled at the side of his throat.

In a flash, he flipped us over and pinned me to the ground. Enraged, I snarled and snapped up at his neck, struggling against him.

To no avail.

I didn't have him, after all. Far from it. Instead, he had me exactly where he wanted me.

I should have walked away while I had the chance. Everything about him—his voice, his scent, his eyes—had made me weak.

Alpha blood or not, I suddenly realized I never stood a chance.

The fight drained out of me and I felt my body start to shift, melting back into human form. Above me, Reid's wolf form faded too, until I was staring up into wide human eyes.

I wasn't struggling any more. The shock of transformation drained me of any fight I had left.

At any rate, he'd won.

He had me pinned. His bare skin was hot against mine.

In a rush, I remembered why it wasn't a good idea to shift into wolf form wearing clothes. There were probably torn pieces of clothing littering the grass all around us.

Those were my new jeans!

It was a minor annoyance in my current position, but still.

The silver in his eyes faded to their usual dark gray, though they were still burning with heat. The expression of desire on his face was one I remembered well.

Our mouths were mere inches apart.

Involuntarily, I licked my lips, and his gaze dropped immediately to my mouth.

He looked like he'd forgotten why we were tangled together like this.

He wasn't making any move to get up, though. And I wasn't making any effort to push him off me.

I could barely feel the grass underneath us anymore, or see the starlit sky above.

I was consumed with the feel of his body on top of mine. We'd been here a thousand times before.

My body remembered it vividly, even if the rest of me had desperately tried to forget.

He drew his arms up until they rested on either side of my head.

One of his hands found my throat and traced the skin there. He slid his fingers through my hair, tilted my head up, and leaned close so that his hair fell down and tickled my shoulders.

When he brushed his lips against mine, I shivered, my lips parting slightly.

He groaned and exhaled against my mouth, deepening the kiss and pressing down against me.

Heat curled in my stomach and I slid my calves against his. Taking advantage of his distraction, I rolled us over so that I straddled him, before leaning back down and kissing him deeply.

When we broke apart, I stared at him, a million thoughts swirling in my head.

What am I doing? God, I've missed this.

He lay there, chuckling. "Alpha."

Judging by his wide smile, he wasn't mad about me flipping us and taking the dominant position. I brushed the hair off his face and ran my hands down his chest and over his arms. He was breathing heavily, looking up at me with something akin to awe.

A small part of me wondered if he'd known this was going to happen. An even bigger part of me screamed to get off him before I did something we would both regret.

His hands wrapped themselves firmly around my hips and I snapped back to the moment.

He was waiting for me to make the call.

Screw it, I thought.

In for a penny, in for a pound.

My fingers tangled in his hair and I dragged him up to meet me in another messy kiss.

CHAPTER 6
REID

Our fight had gone in my favor. Just as I knew it would.

Allara was still fiercely strong, and faster than any of the other women in the pack, but I had the edge of determination and raw strength on my side.

And a point to prove.

Kissing her hadn't been part of my game plan, though.

It's been too long, the wolf in me snarled. *Take her, right now.*

Her hands threaded into my hair and she pulled me up toward her again.

I went willingly.

No hair pulling. I wound my arms tightly around her as she kissed me.

A surge of desire caught me, and I moved her off me, jumped up and then pulled her to her feet. I lifted her against me and she instantly wrapped her legs around my waist, holding on like a limpet as I carried her to her patio door. After a little fumbling to find the handle, I managed to open the door one handed and carry her inside.

The tiny shred of reason left inside me screamed at me to stop, to back away right now, leave. This wasn't meant to happen.

This was the *one thing* that wasn't meant to happen. Every second I held her in my arms, I was breaking down all the barriers that had kept me apart from her.

Barriers I knew had been put in place for a reason. I had agreed, hadn't I?

She wasn't meant for me. I knew that. She never had been.

But if we kept going like this, tonight, then the strings that had once tied us together would be hopelessly tangled again. *And this time, we might never be able to unravel them.*

Once my shifter impulses had kicked in, red mist had descended. Even though we hadn't been near each other for years, my body reacted to her touch as if no time had passed.

Like we were a mated pair. Soul-bonded.

There was only one direction this was heading in and it was a direction I couldn't continue to travel.

And yet, I was powerless to stop.

It had been so long since I felt whole. Five long and lonely years.

We stumbled through her dark condo and I pressed her up against every surface we passed: her kitchen counter, the back of her couch, a nearby wall. She nipped at the skin between my shoulder and neck and I growled with impatience before finally pushing her up against the door she whispered belonged to her bedroom.

She lowered her legs to the floor. I pinned her there as she shivered and gazed up at me. Her pupils were dark, and even in the low light I could tell that her lips were swollen from my kisses.

"I've missed you." The words tumbled out before I could stop them.

Without giving her a chance to register what I'd said, I leaned in and captured her lips again, delving into her mouth without restraint.

The heat building between our dampening skin would have overwhelmed an ordinary human, but it only intensified our desire for each other.

Her scent was driving me crazy. The smell of her shampoo was different, but underneath it she was still Allara. *My* Allara.

I pressed my nose against her neck and growled, scraping my teeth over her sensitive flesh just to feel her pulse skittering. Her legs trembled, like she would collapse if I weren't holding her against me.

She opened the door and drew me in to her bedroom, urging me forward until the back of her legs hit the mattress. Then she swiveled and pushed at my chest, and I sprawled out backwards on top of her bed. She crawled on top of me, her long, gorgeous hair pooling on either side of me, and she took my lower lip between her teeth and bit down, none-too-gently.

I groaned and rolled on top of her. My hands slipped around her waist, and I pulled her up, inch my inch, not stopping until my cock slipped deeply inside her. I'd wanted to do that from the moment I stepped into that dingy city bar.

I'd waited five years. There was no time for finesse.

She gasped and tightened around me so sweetly I almost finished right then and there. But I clenched my jaw and focused on the beauty of her face. I wasn't coming without her.

The room around us spun as I began to move, riding her thrusts as she countered mine.

In that moment, everything vanished from my head in the blink of an eye: the pack, my mission, Jaime. None of it felt real.

Nothing else mattered. Only her.

She hooked her ankles behind me and urged me deeper, panting in my ear. My desire for her was overwhelming, and I buried my face into her neck and gave myself over to it completely, absorbing everything: the taste of her skin, the feel of her perfect body, the softness of her hair, and the look of wanton bliss in her eyes.

We had been here countless times. I could pick out her scent from a thousand. The feeling of her mouth against mine was one I remembered well.

She had been locked in my head for years, in a hundred memories, a thousand tiny moments that took on a much greater significance after she was gone.

I'd replayed my memories of her when she was like this over and over in my head. This was real. Every memory I had of her paled in comparison to the real woman lying beneath me, and the ecstasy of having her with me again.

And then her breath hitched, and I knew she was close. I wanted to hear that keening cry, feel her spasm around me.

I grabbed her hips and tilted her until she moaned, then I sunk into her as deeply as I could, over and over again. Until she was crying out my name and sucking me into orgasm with her.

I groaned as I spilled myself inside her, feeling the wetness of her tears on my cheek as her pussy spasmed around me and we both fell into perfect bliss.

CHAPTER 7

ALLARA

I rolled over in bed and felt the unfamiliar weight of another person lying next to me.

Well. Not quite unfamiliar.

I'd had more than a few dreams like this, in the hazy moments between sleeping and waking. I smiled sleepily and pressed up close against his back until my body was flush with his, inhaling that gorgeous scent.

Reid.

As I began to wake up properly, it all came flooding back.

Last night. The fight. And then we...

Ah, shit.

Twisting away from him, I yanked the covers back and stumbled out of bed, groping around on the floor for my robe.

I cursed myself for being so stupid, for letting him *get* to me like that. No matter how carefully I stepped, it seemed I couldn't help myself when it came to him.

You helped yourself last night, said a voice in my head that sounded suspiciously like Penny's all-knowing tone.

I grimaced at the memory. On Sunday afternoon, I'd swung by the diner to grab a coffee and fill her in on Reid's sudden reappearance, followed by the disastrous meal we had shared there the night before.

Penny was one of the few people in my new life who knew the truth about who I was and where I'd come from.

This had made explaining the whole *Reid* thing easier in some ways, and much, *much* harder in others.

"So, he's... what? An ex-boyfriend of yours?"

I nodded, stirring my coffee. "I guess you could say that."

Penny's expression grew contemplative. "That explains the weird tension, then. Wait—I thought shifters mated for life?"

I cringed. "He's not my mate. He's just Reid."

"Huh." Penny looked skeptical. "If you say so..."

I'd changed the subject and instead regaled her with my bar encounter with the creep who had harassed Tammy. Penny seemed to take the hint, though I could tell she had a million questions hovering on the tip of her tongue.

Not that I was likely to have the answers for her.

I thought I'd known where I stood. Now, it was like the ground beneath me had crumbled away, and I stood at the edge of a cliff, looking down at the jagged rocks below.

When I walked out of the diner last night, I had wondered if Reid's and my brief reunion inside the bar was the last we would see of each other.

I'd had no plans of returning to the pack until he dropped back into my life, after all. At some point, I would probably have visited the pack briefly, to pay my respects to Dad, but up until yesterday, the thought of seeing Reid again had been too painful to contemplate.

Perhaps, I thought, he would take me at face value and give up.

It seemed hopelessly naïve in the cold light of day. Reid wasn't the type to give up on anything that truly mattered.

Like me seeing my dad before he died, obviously.

I stared down at Reid's sleeping form, lost in thought. His brown hair lay fanned out over my pillows, his face buried between them. A heavy sleeper, just like I remembered.

The smooth planes of his back were toned and lithe, although he had filled out since I'd last seen him. Having now reached his physical prime, he'd lost the rangy appearance of a young wolf shifter, and fully come into his adult power.

He looked strange in my little apartment bedroom, like a puzzle piece that didn't quite fit.

Shaking away my confusing thoughts, I grabbed a towel from the linen cupboard and, after a second's hesitation, fresh clothes. I would change in the bathroom.

I was better off leaving him to his own devices while I attempted to pull myself together.

After my shower, I made coffee and toast, curled up at my kitchen table, and waited for him to make an appearance.

It was a little after eight when my bedroom door finally opened, and he padded into the kitchen. Steam trailed in through the open door; he was wearing one of my towels slung loosely around his hips. Water droplets ran down his neck in an obscenely distracting manner. He flashed a grin and shook out his hair, sending water everywhere. He scrubbed at the back of his head with one careless hand.

"Ugh." I hated when he did that.

I only remembered how much I hated it as he was *doing* it.

I kind of regretted making him a coffee now.

His grin widened. Unrepentant, he stole a piece of toast from the plate in front of me and chewed happily, picking up the coffee mug I pushed across the table at him, and wandered back into my bedroom.

The worst part of all of this?

He *knew* that he had me exactly where he wanted me.

It was imperative I return with him now. It was written into our biology, in the shifter blood running through our veins. A promise that couldn't be broken.

I couldn't decide how I felt about that.

I knew one thing for sure: I should never have accepted his stupid challenge in the first place.

Groaning to myself, I put my head in my hands. Last night had been such a mistake.

Now that he'd given me a taste of what we used to have, walking away at the end of all this was going to be so much harder.

He would just repeat what he did last time, and stroll off without a care in the world. I would be left to pick up the pieces. Again.

There was nothing to do about it now, though. I had to see this thing out to the bitter end.

~

"HAVEN'T you missed it at all?"

Reid's voice startled me out of my reverie. I'd been staring out the truck window, watching the skyscrapers turn into suburbs as we reached the edge of the city, before finally giving way to open farmland.

I turned to him.

"Missed what?" I said, though I already knew.

His hands flexed on the steering wheel. His eyes were fixed on the open road. "Home. The pack."

Of course. Before I came here, it was all I'd ever known.

"Not so much anymore," I said. I pulled the sleeves of my sweater down over my hands and hugged myself. "Feels like a long time ago."

It wasn't a total lie. It *did* feel like a long time ago. I had found new people to protect in the city; in some ways, they had almost become my new pack.

He glanced at me. "You cold?"

I shook my head. "No, this truck has shitty insulation, which you still haven't fixed. Don't think I haven't noticed."

It was a bullshit answer and we both knew it. Wolf shifters ran hot; we didn't need the kind of protection from icy weather that ordinary humans did.

"It does! You never..." His face fell, and his expression shuttered. "You never shut up about it."

A weighty silence followed his words.

Our past together lurked around every corner, and we kept slamming into it like a brick wall.

I rubbed the cashmere weave of my sweater between finger and thumb. It wasn't practical for where we were going, but I hadn't taken much stuff with me when I left all those years ago. Most of my clothes were lightweight now. Sneakers and tank tops were much better for a crowded city.

I thought about Reid's question.

Maybe I'd done a better job than I thought of seeming above it all, like I couldn't care less whether he came or went.

Maybe he truly believed I had moved on from my old life with the pack.

Moved on from him.

I had, right?

"Coming back with you... it doesn't mean I'm staying," I heard myself say. "You do know that, right?"

His face turned grave. "I know."

The fields were disappearing outside the windows. We were nearing the edge of the forest now. I caught sight of the first redwoods up ahead of us, and my heart clenched with a queasy mixture of anticipation and dread.

Out of the corner of my eye, I glanced at Reid, but his focus had turned back to the road.

Although I would never admit it to him in a million years, I was comforted by his presence. The only thing worse than my current predicament would be having to face the pack alone.

The redwoods began to thicken, and the winter sun shone dimly through the trees as we drove. The woods were small and spaced out here; some were barely seven feet tall.

The trees at the heart of the forest were giants. They stood tall enough that you could barely see the tops of them, and their branches seemed to stretch out for miles, forming a leafy canopy overhead thick enough in places to block out the stars.

"Stick close," Reid said suddenly. "When we arrive, stay near me, okay? I'll take you straight to your dad."

There was tension in his voice that startled me. I didn't understand or appreciate his tone, but I nodded nonetheless.

Maybe things back home really had changed?

Did he think I was in danger?

"What's up with Jaime, anyway?" I asked, to change the subject. "You said he couldn't be trusted. Why?"

Reid's face darkened. He was silent for a long moment, like he was choosing his words carefully.

"He wants to... expand our territories." His brow furrowed as he stared at the open road ahead of us. The snow-topped mountains loomed in the distance, blue and hazy. "Roll the border out, right across the creek. He wants to take land all the way out to the plains. Once he becomes Alpha, he's planning to start a turf war in every direction."

"What?" My heart began to pound. "He wants to push the Ferrers pack off their land? And the Thornwoods? That's crazy!"

The neighboring packs had lived in peace with ours for as long as I could remember.

"I know." Reid's jaw clenched. "Even if we had the numbers... it's a suicide mission."

I nodded grimly. Not to mention the fact that we would be betraying the trust of people we knew. Our allies. Packs that we'd fought shoulder to shoulder alongside during countless turf wars in the past.

Strange, I thought, how I've already slipped back into thinking of the pack as ours.

And now Jaime wanted to destroy our pack? Destroy everything my dad had built, in an ill-considered and bloodthirsty quest for dominion?

"How do you know all this?" I asked.

I couldn't imagine Jaime revealing his plans willingly, and to *Reid*, of all people.

They had never seen eye to eye. As the son of the pack's Beta, Jaime was a high-ranking male in the pack's hierarchy. Reid was an unknown element, an outsider who, in the eyes of some, had unsettled the natural order of things when he waltzed in and started dating the Alpha's daughter.

When we were young, Reid had been stronger and faster than the others, and everyone knew it. As a foundling, no-one knew Reid's true heritage, but I always assumed he came from an Alpha line. He was huge in wolf form, and protective as all get out. Not to mention loyal, too.

Jaime had challenged him to more than one fight over the years, usually over something petty and stupid. Reid had always had the good sense to refuse.

The notion that Reid was now somehow privy to Jaime's plans seemed absurd.

Still, what do I know? They might be best pals, now.

Maybe Jaime was planning on making Reid his Beta. I'd been away for a long time, after all.

I almost laughed at the ridiculousness of the image. Things might have changed, but they couldn't have changed *that* much.

"About a month ago, I overheard Jason talking to Paul," Reid said.

"About Jaime, and his plans. They'd both tried to tell him how insane it was, apparently, but he wouldn't listen."

That made more sense. Jason was Jaime's best friend. Paul was a couple of years younger, but he had followed the two of them around like a puppy for as long as I could remember.

It hadn't always been that way. Once upon a time, Jason and Reid had been like brothers.

Reid, Jason, Kara and me.

When we were kids, it was just the four of us... our own little pack.

That was a long time ago.

Things were very different now.

"The Thornwoods would retaliate," I said. "They'd go upstate, get help from one of the bigger packs. Maybe even the State Chapter." I tried to keep the panic out of my voice, but I could hear it, nonetheless. "All the peace treaties would be dust. We'd be wiped out!"

"Allara." Reid took one hand off the steering wheel, grabbed my hand, and squeezed it. "*Listen* to me. I know. That's why I came to bring you back. I realize...I realize this isn't what you want. I would have let you be if I could. But the pack needs you right now."

I need you.

His unspoken words echoed in my head and I sighed with frustration. Why did he make me feel like this—as if I knew what he was thinking and feeling as well as I knew my own mind?

Just like last night, I was misinterpreting things again. Filling in the blanks, equipping him with motivations that might not even be accurate.

"Does Dad know?" I asked.

Reid's mouth twisted. He tapped his fingers against the driving wheel and wouldn't meet my eyes. "No."

Something dawned on me. As I put the pieces together, my feelings of despair grew.

"He's been ill for a while, hasn't he?"

He sighed. "Yes. I'm sorry."

I knew that learning the truth about Jaime would break my dad's heart.

Reid had kept that painful news from him, apparently. For better or worse.

"Thank you for sparing Dad that information."

Reid nodded and I turned to stare out the window.

I had to think fast. It wouldn't be long before we arrived. The trees we passed were taller and denser now, and the air had taken on a familiar dim, misty quality. Shafts of sunlight pierced through the branches and lit up patches of undergrowth as we rumbled along.

"Would the pack stand behind Jaime?" I asked. "Some of them might agree with him."

Reid's brow creased, and he shook his head. "I don't know. Some folks, maybe. But most of them would realize that it's total lunacy."

I exhaled shakily. For the first time since we got in the truck, Reid turned his head and met my eyes properly.

"Allara, you and I both know we won't have a choice. Once Jaime becomes Alpha, he can exert his will over the pack. They'll have to do what he says, even if..."

"It kills them," I finished.

That was how it worked. I'd never appreciated how terrifying the prospect was before, nor how easily the power could be abused.

Maybe because Dad, for all his faults, would never dream of leading his pack into danger. Every single decision he made considered pack safety and happiness first and foremost.

I swallowed. *Except when it comes to me, I guess.*

Reid was silent for the rest of the journey. When the track curved to the left, winding off the main road, he glanced at me.

"You ready?"

"Yeah," I lied.

The first rooftops began to peek through the trees. We passed trucks parked up on both sides of the track, and the tarmac road gave way to dirt.

I tried without much success to quell the flutter of nerves in my stomach.

Reid pulled up outside his house and turned the key to cut the engine.

The truck suddenly felt way too still and silent for my liking.

Although I was eager for a chance to stretch my legs after the long journey, I took my time opening the passenger door and climbing out.

Our arrival had not gone unnoticed. People came out of the meeting house across the street, stopping in their tracks to stare at us.

Who was I kidding?

They stared at *me*.

Their eyes burned into the back of my head as I slammed the door of Reid's truck louder than I needed to. I mostly kept my head down, but still noticed some familiar faces in amongst the gathering crowd.

On the wide porch of the Briars' house, Jason stood watching us, his sister Kara by his side.

My mouth twitched as I noticed that their faces were perfect mirror images of shock.

I couldn't help but feel the ghost of something at the sight of Kara. A feeling that was akin to regret.

She had been my closest childhood friend. I was an only child, the lonely daughter of the Alpha wolf. Most of the other children had treated me with respect, but they never forgot who I was, or what I was destined to be. They weren't cold to me, but they weren't warm, either.

Except Kara. We had been almost sisters when we were kids, joined at the hip.

Then Reid came along, and the four of us had hung around for a little while. Reid, Jason, Kara and I, making forts in the woods, pranking the other kids, and causing all kinds of trouble.

And then Mom died.

I'd withdrawn from Kara, just like I had from practically everything and everyone else.

I spotted Luke, who had been a kid the last time I saw him. He was now a gangly teenager. He reminded me a little of Reid at the same age, standing in the awkward fashion of someone who wasn't yet certain how to arrange their long limbs.

One by one, everyone in the immediate vicinity fell silent. Every face turned toward me.

Watching. Waiting, no doubt, to see what I would do next.

Run away? Again?

It seemed like the most attractive option, albeit a highly impractical one at this moment.

Instead, I lifted my head high, and straightened my spine, hearing my dad's voice float to the surface of my mind from some long-forgotten memory.

Alpha wolves do not bow to anyone, Allara.

I had to face this situation head on. I had to act like I couldn't care less about the stir my appearance had created.

Easier said than done.

A warm hand landed around my shoulders, a firm, steady pressure that eased the nervous tension a little.

Reid.

He was a solid presence by my side. He turned me slightly, shielding me from prying eyes with his body.

"Show's over, folks!" he called out, waving a hand at the audience we'd gathered. A few more curious glances shot my way, then the crowd began to disperse, murmuring amongst themselves.

After a couple of minutes, we were alone on the dirt road that ran straight through the center of the small village.

Our small village.

I stepped away from Reid, and his hand fell back to his side.

His face fell, too.

"I'll see you later?" I said, before I could stop myself.

He brightened and gave me a crooked smile. "Definitely."

My old house lay at the end of the street, just around the corner. It was set back a little from the other houses, down a small gravel path.

When I reached the house, the long timber beams supporting the overhanging porch, and the swing where I used to sit with Reid… everything seemed exactly the same.

Just like I never left.

There was a light in the small window at the top of the house. The attic, where my dad's study had been. Was it still his study? Or was he too ill to do any work there, anymore?

He had always kept a lamp burning there all through the night. One time, I asked him why. I had been very small and wanted him to keep talking to me so I didn't have to go to sleep.

"Because, Allie," he'd said as he tucked the blanket up under my chin and smoothed the covers beneath his hands. "Sometimes even Daddy has to sleep. And this way, my lamp can keep watch over the whole pack, and keep everyone safe."

"Like a lighthouse?" I asked.

"Just like a lighthouse." He kissed my forehead. "Exactly. It's my job to protect everyone in this pack, honey. And, one day, it will be yours."

I snuggled down under the covers. "Goodnight, Daddy."

"Goodnight, Allara. Sweet dreams."

The memory faded away, and my happiness at the familiar sight mingled with dread at the thought of what I would find up in that attic room.

CHAPTER 8
ALLARA

Before I could talk myself out of what I had to do, I strode up to the porch and fumbled in the pocket of my jeans, drawing out the small key I'd found buried in the bottom drawer of my closet back in the city.

A lump formed in my throat as I slid it into the lock and turned the handle.

Maybe he changed the locks.

The door opened easily. I stepped inside, inhaling the familiar smell of pine leaves, smoke, and... family.

My chest grew tight. I dug my nails into my palm to prevent tears from falling.

Why had I stayed away so long?

Was the hurt back then worth alienating myself from everything I had ever known and loved?

I could barely even swallow. My throat ached at holding back the emotion.

The hallway was dimly lit. As I closed the door behind me, taking care to be quiet, a woman appeared at the top of the stairs.

Rachel. My mom's oldest friend. The woman who'd taken Reid in, raised him practically as her own child. She'd always had my back.

After Mom died, she'd been the only one to defend my relationship with Reid. On one memorable occasion, she had even argued with my dad about it.

He'd thought we were too young to be spending so much time together, and she had reminded him sharply of the way he and Mother were at that age.

After that, he never brought it up again.

"Allara?" She blinked at me, looking as dumbfounded as everyone else in the village.

I raised my hand in greeting and smiled at her weakly.

She seemed to gather herself together, and raced down the stairs, sweeping me into a rib-cracking hug before pulling back to look me over like she couldn't believe her eyes.

"What—how—*when* did you get back?"

"Whoa!" I said, grinning. "Slow down! Just now, I swear. I came straight here."

Her eyes filled with happiness. "Reid found you, then."

I dropped my gaze and untangled myself gently from her embrace. "Yeah."

So, she had known he was coming to look for me.

It occurred to me that I didn't know whether Reid had acted alone. Had he confided in anyone about his plans for bringing me home? Rachel had clearly suspected it, at least.

Was she the only one?

"Your father's upstairs." Her hand pressed against mine, holding tight. "He's... I'm so sorry, Allara. He's very ill."

"Reid told me already." I blinked back a tidal wave of emotions before they threatened to spill over, determined to meet her kind, familiar gaze with calm rather than panic. "Can I see him?"

"Of course, honey." She put her hand on my elbow and led me into the kitchen. "You can take him his glass of water. He needs to take his medication, and he hides the pills otherwise."

I snorted despite myself and grabbed a glass from the cupboard before filling it up.

That sounds like Dad, alright.

Trying to keep my breathing steady, I climbed up the stairs with the glass in my hand. Once I reached the landing, I spared a glance at my old bedroom door.

Had he kept it as it was? Or had he cleared it out?

I couldn't bring myself to peek inside. I didn't particularly like either of those options.

The narrow stairs that led up to the top bedroom were fitted with a stair-rail that hadn't been there when I left. I knocked once on the door, and then pushed it open softly.

"Rachel?" A voice, frailer and quieter than I remembered, floated over from the other side of the room. "That you?"

I hadn't been allowed into the attic much as a child. The adults had been afraid I might overhear something, a pack secret that wasn't meant for a child's ears. My dad and his Beta, Terry, would work in here; maps were often pinned to the walls, plans weighted to the coffee table, almanacs stacked up on the sideboard as they made plans each new year.

Resolving feuds, managing supply runs, chairing council meetings, negotiating trade deals: in the pack, everything was done with the changing seasons, drafted into existence as frost coated the windowpanes, golden leaves blustered through the streets, or the first buds of spring curled open on the branches outside.

When Mom died, Dad had taken to sleeping up here.

He'd never come back down. Not really.

I inhaled sharply as pain squeezed my ribs. He was sitting near the window, reclining in his favorite armchair. He was propped up on a stack of pillows. An old TV set buzzed faintly in the background. A stack of newspapers rested on the coffee table beside him. I'd clearly just woken him.

My chest tightened. "Hey, Dad."

He turned, startled. His sudden recognition felt like the clouds parting to reveal the sun.

"Allara?"

The newspaper on his lap slid onto the floor. I approached him slowly, picked it up and placed it on his unmade bed.

I'm being too cautious. Relax. If your body language conveys tension, he'll sense it.

Hell, he *taught you that.*

He looked up at me, blinking.

I gave him a faint smile. "Yeah, it's me."

He angled his head to get a proper look at me. He had aged so much since I'd last seen him. His hair had almost entirely turned white, and his body was completely dwarfed by the chair he sat in.

There was barely an echo of the strong man in the prime of his life that I knew as a little girl. The intervening years, and the losses they brought with them, had obviously taken a great toll on him.

"It's really you, isn't it?" He reached out and touched my hair. His touch was as light as the brush of a cobweb. "After all this time, the prodigal daughter returns."

"Reid brought me home," I heard myself say.

I was still reeling from the sight of my father like this. The proud Alpha wolf he had once been still lurked somewhere behind those clouded eyes.

It must. He can't be gone from me already.

At the mention of Reid's name, my father sighed deeply. "Ah, yes. Of course."

I bristled. Surely, he couldn't be holding onto his old grudges even now?

A thousand defensive comments swirled in my head. Before I could express any of them, however, my father spoke again.

"Allara." He drew a deep, shuddering breath, looking like it took all his energy to do so. "I owe you an apology."

I went still. *What?*

Whatever I'd been expecting, it wasn't *that.*

"Five years ago," he continued. "You left us. I know it was because of me."

He paused and gave a couple of great, hacking coughs. I passed the glass of water over to him, looking around for his medication.

"Dad, it's fine. Just rest, okay?"

"No." He batted my hands away, taking the glass but refusing to drink. "I'm fine."

"You're not fine!" *So stubborn.* Now I remembered where I got it from. "You need to save your strength."

"I've *been* saving it." He met my eyes. "For this. For you, Allara. I had to talk to you. Before..."

He trailed off. His gaze turned inward, like he was looking at something I couldn't see.

I took a seat in the easy chair opposite him, giving him a chance to gather his thoughts.

"I never meant to make you feel like you didn't belong here," he murmured, so quiet that I had to lean forward to hear him. "I think about the night you left all the time. I think about the choices I made back then..."

"Like announcing Jaime as your successor?"

He looked up. His eyes were steel blue, piercing. The clouds vanished. In that moment, for a few seconds at least, he looked like his old, strong self.

"Being a leader is about strategy, Allara," he said, leaning back and folding his hands together. "I had to think about the pack. I didn't know whether they would accept you as my successor. A woman taking the role of Alpha... it isn't unheard of, but in these parts?"

As much as his reasoning made sense, my voice still trembled with anger as I said, "So, you—what? Just decided to keep me out of the loop altogether?"

"I never kept you out of anything!" he barked, refusing to meet my eyes. Instead, he stared beyond me, gazing out of the window at the forest. "I couldn't *reach* you, Allara. As much as I wanted to. I... I didn't know how."

For the first time, I saw our situation through new eyes. Me and Reid grew close after Mom died. Dad had withdrawn from me, sure. But I'd pulled away from him, too.

"Terry and I talked it over. After your mom..." He hung his head. We'd never properly spoken about her death. I could sense that wasn't going to change, even now. "You seemed so lost, Allie. You weren't ready for the responsibility."

"And Jaime?" I asked. "You thought Jaime could take on that responsibility?"

My father's face softened. "It wasn't an either-or situation. I thought he would be a good match for you, when the time came."

Confusion rose in me. "So, you thought that by naming Jaime as your successor, I would eventually become his mate?"

My mouth twisted. On paper, it did sound like a neat solution. The ideal way to appease those in the pack who wanted a male Alpha, *and* those who wanted a leader with actual Alpha blood.

A perfect match.

Too bad I'd refused to play along.

He met my eyes and it was as though his piercing gaze reached into my mind and turned over my thoughts, one by one.

"I wanted you to step up, Allara. You and Jaime had the potential to lead the pack together, side by side. I wanted you to think about your future here."

A new thought nudged at the back of my mind, hazy at first, before it slid abruptly into focus.

"You ordered Reid to end things with me," I whispered. "Didn't you?"

"Like I said..." He leaned forward, placing his trembling hand over mine. "I'm *sorry*."

A jumble of emotions threatened to overwhelm me as I sat there in silence and tried to make sense of it all.

For so many years, I'd avoided thinking about that night; the moment Reid's words had washed over me and broken me apart, piece by piece.

At the time I had been in shock, unable to think straight. The breakup had seemed to come totally out of the blue. It had left me reeling, wondering if there had been signs of his fading affection that I'd missed.

I recalled the things he said that night with excruciating clarity.

Even all these years later, those words had jagged edges; they cut me just as sharply as they had the first time I'd heard them.

We can't be together anymore. I should never have let it get this far.

You had to know... we were never going to last forever.

Allara, I'm doing this for you.

Maybe he really *had* done it for me.

Or... done what he *thought* was the best thing for me.

"The boy wasn't easy to convince, Allara."

My dad's words broke through my reverie.. He sat there, gazing at me. His eyes were overcast once more, full of regret.

"I tried everything I could think of to make him see reason." He stared at the television, but I knew he wasn't really seeing the screen. "I offered him money. That didn't work. Then I threatened him."

My lips parted a little, but no words came out.

A threat?

My dad shook his head. "I'm not proud of it. But still he wouldn't budge. I gave him the chance to pack up, go start a new life somewhere, far away. He wouldn't take any of it."

I swallowed hard, unable to speak.

That sounded like Reid all right.

If my dad had thought any of those options would sway Reid, then he didn't know him at all. Reid didn't care about money, and he was afraid of nothing.

"Finally, I asked him to consider your future," my dad whispered. "As the Alpha's daughter, I told him that you had certain... responsibilities. That, sooner or later, you were going to have to make a choice."

A choice. Between the pack, and Reid.

"You were worried I would choose wrong," I said softly.

He nodded. "I was. And I had every reason, Allara. I couldn't know for certain whether or not you would put the pack's welfare first."

I looked away from him, and watched the bare branches of the tree outside tapping against the glass. "I guess we'll never know what I may or may not have done. But, without him..."

The pack wasn't worth leading. There wasn't anything here worth staying for.

When I'd been cast adrift after my mother had died, he was the one who found me and pulled me back to shore. I couldn't envisage life here without him.

My father seemed to catch the words I left unsaid, because he simply nodded, regret etched across his face.

He'd tried to force my hand, and he'd lost everything. We both had.

"I made a mistake, Allara." He leaned forward and took my hand in both of his. "I didn't understand the depth of your feelings for him. That was *my* failing, not yours."

I sniffed and wiped at my face with my cuff sleeve.

"Your mother and I..." The ghost of a smile flickered across his face. "Well, I knew it from the moment I met her that I would do whatever it took to keep her safe. That I could never be without her. When you find your mate, you *know*."

"I could never be with Jaime," I said, feeling the need to explain myself. "There was no one else. Only Reid."

"Allie," he said, pulling me forward with a surprising amount of strength to gather me up into a hug. "I'm sorry."

"I'm sorry for leaving," I mumbled into his shoulder, realizing that, despite the fact he'd tried to manipulate my life, I'd ended up proving him right. That the pack wasn't the most important part of my life. Reid was.

We broke apart and I wiped at the tears on my cheeks.

"I put you in an impossible position," he said, brushing the hair out of my face and giving me a chagrined smile. "And, for what it's worth, I'm proud of all you have accomplished, out there on your own."

I frowned. "How do you know what I've accomplished? You haven't..."

I stopped. Of course, he had kept an eye on me. I was pack. I was the Alpha's daughter. There's no way they'd have just let me disappear, without keeping some kind of tabs on me.

I wasn't sure whether to be grateful or annoyed that maybe I hadn't been as alone all these years as I had thought.

Tears sprouted, and even then, I couldn't tell what emotion was foremost in my mind. Eventually I rubbed my eyes and shook my head. Given my tears, I must have made an unappealing picture, but my dad didn't comment on it.

"You're proud of the bartending on the weekends? Assistant teaching? Hardly a glittering career, Dad," I managed to say.

"It's all yours, though." His eyes twinkled. "My little lone wolf. You must've learned some mean cocktail recipes, at least."

I laughed. "Totally."

"You know who else would be proud of you?" Dad's voice trembled, but he continued regardless. "Your mom. She loved you very much."

I gave a shaky nod. I worried that if I spoke in that moment, I would start bawling again.

"You're my daughter, Allara." My dad brought my head forward and touched our foreheads together. "My true heir. I neglected you when you needed me, and I'm sorrier for it than I can say. I want to make things right between us while I still can."

The weight of hurt... of betrayal, fell away, leaving me light. I let out a long breath.

"You already have, Dad."

With a peaceful smile, he fell into a doze. I left him and tiptoed back downstairs to find Rachel.

I settled in one of the living room armchairs with a mug of cocoa and tucked my feet up beneath me.

Rachel sat opposite. She took a careful sip from her own mug and fixed me with an unreadable expression.

Although I could barely admit it, even to myself, I wished Reid were here. It might help to diffuse the tension in the room.

"It's good to see you," I said. "It's been too long."

"Five years too long." Her eyebrows drew together as she frowned. "I called you, Allie. Several times. You never picked up."

"I'm sorry." I let out a shaky breath. "I... I changed my phone. I needed a clean break, Rachel. I never got your messages, sorry. I just... had to leave it all behind."

She set her mug down carefully on the coffee table and folded her hands in her lap with a heavy sigh. "You never truly turned your back though, did you Allie?"

I stared down at the mug in my hands, my heart thumping. "What makes you say that?"

"Well, it's obvious." Rachel's voice was surprisingly gentle. I looked up, forcing myself to look her in the eye. "Reid is your mate."

Your mate.

The two words reverberated through me until they were all I could hear.

I stared blindly at the mantel, looking at the photographs set out on display there. Reid and I when we were kids. Rachel and I baking a cake, covered in frosting. My dad, looking about thirty years younger, glowing, with his arms wrapped around my mom.

Rachel had probably put them there. Dad didn't have any photos of Mom in the house when I lived here.

"That's what Dad said. Well, implied," I said, feeling proud of the fact my voice didn't wobble. "But... Reid broke up with me, Rachel. Dad told him to do it. I know that now. But... I thought it wasn't possible to walk away from your mate like that. If you were truly bound together, I mean."

"Oh, Allie." Rachel shook her head at me, just like she used to do when I was ten and she caught me skipping out on homework to go play in the woods. "You think he walked away? He never did."

A sudden surge of irritation caught hold of me at the knowing smile on her face.

"Uh, yes. He *did*. You weren't there. You didn't see his face. It seemed so *easy* for him."

"And yet," Rachel said softly, "after you left, I was here. I saw the effect it had on him. It was like something inside him just... switched off. I'd never seen him like that before. He barely spoke to anyone, didn't want anything to do with the pack. He just went off by himself. Sometimes he didn't return for days on end."

I absorbed her words slowly.

"I didn't see the point in being here if I couldn't be with him," I said. "I'm sorry."

Rachel nodded, sighing. "I understand that. And I'll bet you he felt just the same."

Now, with hindsight, I was sure she was right, but for me, leaving had been the only way to stay sane.

Then again, if I'd stayed, maybe I could have stopped Jaime from making his plans to destroy our pack.

Hopefully it wasn't too late to stop him now.

RACHEL'S WORDS echoed through my head while I wandered the village, saying a few quick hellos to old friends and acquaintances as

I passed. I kept my conversations brief and didn't answer any questions about where I'd been, or why I'd gone away.

Rachel thought that Reid and I were... mates.

It wasn't an impossibility. Nobody knew why the "fated mates" attraction happened. It didn't happen to every shifter, but it was common enough for our kind that plenty of tales were told of it.

I had heard many, over the years.

They were spoken of around the campfire on lazy summer evenings. The elders told the stories, and the smoke above our heads framed image after image of love, death, and war. Women who had run away from home after pack-meets to chase after the shifter men that they couldn't get out of their heads. Packs turning to bloodshed and violence over a stolen woman, or a broken marriage pact.

Many people said that my mother and father had been fated.

To be honest, they were probably right, though the phenomenon was shrouded in secrecy.

Bonded mates were something only the council could officially determine.

If they had known anything about me and Reid, they'd kept their cards close to their chests, right up until I left.

The only reason I took Rachel's belief to heart was that Rachel was probably the only person in the world who knew Reid almost as well as I did.

CHAPTER 9
ALLARA

I had been seven years old when Reid came to our town.

My dad had leaned down and scooped me up to sit on his shoulders. My mom walked alongside him, explaining something to him in low, urgent tones.

They'd found Reid on the steps of the meeting house, early in the morning.

He was a scruffy, skinny foundling, roughly eight or nine years of age. His hair was a dark, chestnut brown color, and his eyes were a clear gray.

Even though I'd been young, I remembered his eyes the best of all. They had been wide, and full of fear.

At first, he had glared daggers at everyone who dared to come near him. He seemed half-feral; a little cub dropped into the den by who-knew-who.

He wouldn't talk at all for the first few days, although he'd eaten everything put before him with a ravenous hunger.

No-one seemed to know where he had come from or guess at how he'd arrived in the middle of our village.

He couldn't—or wouldn't—answer any of the questions the pack elders asked him, even after he finally started to speak.

The only concrete piece of information that they managed to get out of him was that his name was Reid.

Finally, it was agreed by the council that he should be taken in and cared for until his identity was confirmed, or until the pack he belonged to came back to claim him.

It was decided that he should live with Rachel, who had no children of her own, a spare bedroom, and a gentle manner. He started going to school with the rest of us kids and, after a few months, it was just as though he'd always been here.

Although my father sent out dozens of lines of enquiry, nobody came forward to take him back to wherever he'd come from. Not a whisper from any of the neighboring packs, nor any indication that someone out there was missing a son.

A single shred of evidence arrived one day, three years after Reid came to us. It was via an unmarked envelope, and it contained a handwritten message which simply read:

He is safe here.

As for Reid himself, the strangeness of his arrival was only the beginning.

He grew into a quiet boy who was far more interested in climbing trees and building forts by himself than playfighting with Jaime and the other boys of his age.

Even as a child, it was clear to the pack that he was a shifter. His strength and speed were incomparable to that of a human child. If his agility hadn't been enough of a giveaway, then the way his eyes swirled with silver a few weeks after his twelfth birthday certainly was.

Not long after that, his first shift happened.

Unlike most of the pack, whose fur colors varied between grayish silver and a light, sandy brown, his coat was rich and dark, a deep brown like his hair color. In both wolf and human form, he stood a fraction taller than the other boys, and his pelt was thicker and shaggier, too.

I experienced my own shift a few months later.

In my wolf form, I was quick and deft, and to my delight I was by far the best at clambering up steep riverbanks and wriggling through tiny crevices. The forest around us was like a giant playground, and we reveled in it. The boys were always stronger than me, but far clumsier, with their overlarge paws. On top of this, they had little regard for danger, and their recklessness came back to bite them more often than not.

I couldn't help but smile at the memories this place held for me.

Reid was well liked by most and grew into a strong and dependable man—an asset for a pack of our size, though the unanswered question of Reid's origin continued to haunt us.

Although he never spoke about his life before he'd come to our pack, even to me, I knew that it bothered him somewhere deep down. The pack's adult members accepted him as one of us under strict orders from my father, but I knew that in many ways he would always be seen as an outsider to them.

Their prejudice was on some level instinctive. Sometimes the wires got crossed in the wolf part of our brains; Reid was no enemy to them, but he was no kin, either. They always treated him with respect, but often kept him at a careful distance.

Nobody had to tell me that my father would have never considered Reid to be a suitable match for me.

The Alpha's daughter would never be partnered with a foundling cub from who-knows-where.

It didn't matter to me, or to Reid. Practically from the minute he'd arrived, we'd been inseparable.

"Allie?"

I started, and realized that I had been so deep in my thoughts that I'd wandered right to the edge of the village. I had come upon the small, babbling brook which cut a path through this part of the forest and provided our village with fresh water, straight from the mountains.

Kara crouched by the side of the stream, rinsing out a beautiful piece of cloth the same color of the redwood leaves behind her. Her arms were green too, right up to her elbows, so that it looked like she was wearing gloves. After a second, I realized she was in the process of dying the material. She'd always been an artist; half the blankets in the village had been woven by her.

She stared at me, waiting for a response.

"Oh." I flushed. "Hi, Kara."

"Long time, no see," she said evenly, drawing the cloth out of the water and wringing it. "Reid said you moved to the city."

That's understating things, somewhat.

I inclined my head. "Yeah, I've been away a while, huh?"

She just nodded. Her expression was unreadable. "About your dad... I'm sorry. How's he doing?"

"Thanks." A ripple of sadness swum through me as I recalled the reason for my return. "He's in good spirits, but... he's worried, I think."

Something flickered in Kara's eyes. I sensed that she caught the fullness of my meaning.

So... that must mean things have *been different around here.*

"Must be difficult for him." Heaving the cloth out of the water, she flung it out onto the boulder next to her and sat back on her hands. "I guess we all do what we think is right, in the moment."

She was talking about the succession. Jaime being named my father's heir, ahead of me. As uncomfortable as the topic made me, I knew that I should get the lay of the land from her. Kara was as good a person as any to talk to. She always gave good advice, and I trusted her judgment better than most.

I leaned against a nearby tree and took my chance.

"Has Jason told you anything? About...?"

I didn't need to finish my sentence. Jaime and Jason had been thick as thieves for years now; wherever Jaime went, Jason was sure to follow.

She snorted suddenly. "Nope. You'd think he'd open up to his twin sister, wouldn't you? But no. He's always with Jaime and Paul nowadays. I hardly see him."

That pretty much lined up with what Reid had told me. Still, I couldn't help but wonder whether there was more to the story.

"They've always been best friends, though," I pressed. "Right?"

She shook her head. "It's not that. I can't explain it, but... something's changed here, Allara. Ever since..."

She trailed off.

Right. Ever since I left the pack.

I really wished people would stop reminding me.

"Come to think of it," Kara said suddenly, "there was this one night. A couple of months ago, I came down to the kitchen to get a glass of water. I heard something... weird."

My heart rate picked up, but I forced my voice to remain calm. "Jaime was there?"

"No," Kara said. "*Reid*, of all people. He was talking to my brother... and they weren't exactly keeping their voices down. It sounded like an argument if I'm being honest."

"What did you hear?" I said, too intrigued to pose the question subtly.

She shrugged, shooting me a curious look.

"I couldn't make sense of it. Reid said something about Jaime being... dangerous, I think. Then Jason said...ah..." Her cheeks went pink. "Something about you, actually."

"About me?"

"First, he told Reid to stay out of their business." Kara grimaced.

"That it was none of his concern. And that he was just jealous of Jaime, because, uh, your dad wanted *him* to be with you, and not Reid."

I didn't reply. I was too busy thinking about what my dad had said earlier.

As the Alpha's daughter, you had certain responsibilities.

"Reid left pretty soon after that," Kara said. "I think Jason might have said some other things, about Reid coming here, maybe. About him being a foundling, and not having any family. Stuff like that. But I didn't catch much of that part."

I frowned to myself, thinking.

I couldn't tell Kara about what Jaime planned to do after he became Alpha. It would only put her in danger, and besides, Jason was her twin brother. I didn't want any of my suspicions to fall on the wrong ears.

Jason had always struck me as a decent person, though. He was kind and thoughtful, just like his sister.

"Does Jason really think that?" I asked. "About Reid?"

After all, they had been friends, hadn't they? Once upon a time.

It seemed difficult to square this version of Jason with my dim memories of the two of them.

Back then, it was simple. The sun had always shone, and we were happy.

But we were older now. Supposedly wiser for it, too, though I didn't know how true that was.

Everything was so much more complicated.

"About him being jealous of Jaime? Probably. But not about Reid's parentage." Kara trailed her hand in the flow of water and looked up at me. "No. That's not like him, Allara. That's Jaime all over. It's like the words were coming out of Jason's mouth, but Jaime was saying them. He's gotten to my brother in some way. Jason's under his influence now... and whatever they're up to, it can't be good. I'm sure of it."

CHAPTER 10
REID

I woke with a jolt.

For a few moments, I struggled to remember where I was. The past couple of weeks had been disorientating, and I hadn't slept in this room in a long time.

Looking around, it was as if hundreds of memories patchworked themselves together with my present reality. Allara's quilt spread across the bed, all her old posters covered the walls... it brought me back to a different time.

On the pinboard above the dresser was a postcard from the day we'd spent together at Gold Beach. Just in front of it was the stuffed bear I'd won for her at the carnival when we were sixteen.

The real woman snuggled closer into my chest, forcing me out of my recollections. Even in sleep, she held me close, like she was worried I would disappear.

I stroked her dark tresses out of her face. After a few minutes, Allara's blue eyes blinked open and she gazed at me with a sleepy kind of surprise.

All the events of the previous day seemed to rush back to her, all at once. She extracted herself from my arms and hopped out of bed, pulling her hair up into a messy bun and securing it with a band from around her wrist.

"Allara." I groaned at the rush of cold air and pulled the covers up over my chest. "C'mon, it's way too early. Come back to bed!"

She tucked a loose strand of hair behind her ear and shot me a cheeky grin.

"No, thanks. I'm gonna go see Dad. I thought I could make him a virgin cocktail today. I don't think it's a good idea to give him alcohol, but I thought it might be fun to show him my skills in some way." Smirking, she picked up my flannel shirt off the floor and slipped it on. "Such as they are."

"So, it went well with you guys yesterday, then?" I said, trying to keep my voice light and casual.

After the visit with her father, she'd been distinctly untalkative last night, eating little and saying even less.

I hadn't seen the man himself for some time, but I shoved down my curiosity. Allara didn't need an interrogation from me on top of everything else.

She seemed to be in a better mood today, though. Her eyes brightened as she wrapped my shirt around her body. The sight of her in my clothes always did strange things to me. I managed to ignore the surge of arousal and focus on the conversation.

"Surprisingly, it did!" Her voice was warm as she opened her closet and rifled through the coat hangers, pulling out some of her old clothes. "He explained... a lot. In particular, the stuff that happened around the time I left the pack."

She wouldn't meet my eye, but I caught her drift well enough.

"Oh," I said, and left it at that. For now.

I didn't want to ruin her sunny mood, especially not when things were going so well between the two of us.

Plus, I didn't know how much her dad had told her. *Stuff that happened...*

Stuff about Jaime?

About me?

I desperately wanted to tell her everything about that night, but I knew it had to wait.

Once an agreement was reached, an Alpha's word was binding. Allara's father had been very clear. First, I had to break things off between us, and break her heart in the bargain. Second, I couldn't ever tell her why.

Only when the Alpha died would the pact between us be broken. As much as I didn't want anything to happen to Allara's dad, I did want the truth to come to light, one day.

Not that I was certain how she would react when it did. Maybe she would never forgive me. But at least there wouldn't be any more secrets between us.

I'd lived with them—and their consequences—long enough.

"He said he was proud of me." She smiled at me, looking rueful. "For what, I don't know."

I pillowed my head with my arms and appraised her. A pulse of excitement shot through me when I saw her gaze lingering on my biceps. "So modest."

She threw the sweater she was holding at my head, and I ducked out of the way, cackling with laughter.

Our attention was diverted by a couple of knocks at the bedroom door.

Allara quickly buttoned up my shirt on her, then headed over to the door. She was still giving me the evil eye in between her giggles as she opened the door.

Rachel stood on the threshold. Her face was entirely drained of color.

"Allara," she whispered. "I need you to come upstairs with me right now."

For most of the pack, the death of their Alpha was a once-in-a-lifetime event.

The very oldest members had only been children when Allara's grandfather had died. With one or two exceptions, such as myself, the pack's structure was mostly made up of members from those original families.

By the time Allara had said her last goodbyes and his body had been taken away, we walked outside the Alpha's house and were greeted with quite a spectacle.

Hundreds of candles lined the path leading up to the front door. What looked like the entire pack had assembled outside, huddled into small groups, holding vigil for their fallen leader. They were dressed in black and gray, and tears streaked some of the women's cheeks.

They were waiting for some kind of direction. They wanted to hear what would happen next.

Allara stood beside me, her back straight and her face grim.

She was her father's daughter through and through. It would have been clear, even to an ordinary human, that Alpha blood ran through her veins.

I stood by her side, close enough to see the tension she carried in her shoulders. But then, I knew her better than most. I knew all her little tells, the ways she put on a mask to hide her pain from the world.

She had rifled through the back of her wardrobe and found a simple black dress that had once belonged to her mother. Her face was very pale, but her eyes were dry. She held her head high as she surveyed the waiting crowd.

"My father is gone."

A ripple went through the pack, as though she had thrown a stone into a still pond.

People gasped, and a few cried out. Young children hid their faces against their parents' chests. But most of the pack stood silent and still, ashen-faced.

Every man, woman, and child in the pack—they had all known this was coming for a long time, but that didn't make this moment any easier to bear.

Allara opened her mouth, then closed it again. She lowered her gaze and pressed her lips together hard, obviously fighting grief.

I put my arm around her shoulders and gave her a gentle squeeze, and she looked up at me, her expression beseeching.

"I can take it from here if you want," I murmured, so that only she could hear.

She reached up and slid her hand over mine.

Yes.

"Elder Mason will perform the rites." I raised my voice, so that the entire pack could hear me. My voice echoed through the silent crowd; only the wind in the trees answered. "He has already made the preparations. We gather at noon, at the boneyard."

There was a figure at the edge of the spectators, standing a little apart from the rest of the mourners. Before I finished speaking, he turned and hurried away down the track before vanishing from sight.

Jason, I thought.

Perhaps no one had yet told Jaime the news.

I was sure Jason would be off to do that, now.

I gave a few more parting words to the crowd before guiding Allara back into the house. I shut the door behind us and let out a long breath. I'd always disliked crowds, and it was a relief to be free of the dozens upon dozens of eyes, watching us. More specifically, watching Allara, waiting for answers, most of which she couldn't give.

Allara kept glancing up the stairs. It was like she expected her dad to come walking down them at any moment, hale and hearty.

Part of me wondered whether she was strong enough for what lay ahead.

"Hey, hey." I took her face in my hands and forced her to look at me. "I got you, okay? I got you. I'm right here, I promise."

She nodded and blinked with those blue eyes that always held me so entranced. Her expression wobbled a little, and she flung her arms around my neck, burying her face in my shoulder.

I swept her hair out of the way and kissed the side of her head, just above her ear.

"Don't leave," she mumbled, so quietly I almost missed it.

I drew back and met her eye, tucking a few errant strands of hair back into place.

"I swear upon my ancestors, whoever they might be." I smiled, watching her mouth curl upwards just a little. I cupped her jaw and placed a soft kiss on her parted lips. "I'm not going anywhere."

THE BONEYARD LAY about a half mile from the village, down a narrow gravel track. Carved wooden posts covered with tendrils of ivy marked the trail on either side of us.

Burning tapers signified the entrance, and I shivered as we passed under them.

I wasn't frightened of old spirits that might haunt this place. Those ghost tales were for kids. I knew that the dead had no power over the living, even here.

It was the living folk that concerned me.

One in particular.

A raised platform had been erected around a freshly dug patch of earth. At the graveside, Elder Mason stood with the dusty records book and an ancient looking carved staff. His face was solemn, but other than that, he betrayed no emotion.

There were a few scattered sobs from the people behind us, but the scene was eerily silent otherwise.

Across the circle of mourners, I spotted Jaime's sandy blond head of hair. He caught my eye, and a slow, satisfied smile spread across his face.

My eyes narrowed as I studied him. Did he know that I'd figured him out?

We had sparred often enough in the past, but as hot-headed as he could be, he had always known better than to deepen our enmity. I was young and strong, an asset to the pack. If he drove me out, he would weaken his position considerably, and without false modesty, he and I both knew he would likely weaken the pack, as well.

Once or twice, I'd caught him watching Allara in a manner that made the hairs on the back of my neck stand up. Part of it was attraction, and that part I understood. She had always been gorgeous; no-one could deny that.

But there was something else—a deeper, darker undercurrent to his gaze. I sensed that he wanted to possess her, ensnare her like an animal in a trap.

He needed her lineage to legitimize his claim, but I knew he would destroy her if he had to. He would stop at nothing to secure his power.

Before long, he would have everything he wanted.

He would be Alpha.

If push came to shove, I would leave the pack. I would take Allara to the city and leave everyone behind, everything I'd ever known, in order to protect her.

Once Jaime became Alpha, things wouldn't be safe for her here.

I didn't know how long we had. I hoped that we would be given a few days' grace before we had to make the decision.

I wondered if, after the announcement, Jaime would ask Allara to undertake a bonding ceremony with him and make her his mate without wasting any time.

It seemed unlikely that Allara would agree to anything like that.

My stomach dropped at the thought, nonetheless.

If he lays a finger on her...

I forced down the hot surge of anger as images of Jaime in Allara's bed flashed through my head. Him on top of her...

No. I needed to stop that train of thought immediately.

I turned my attention to back to the ceremony.

"He was beloved by us all," Elder Mason was saying. "A strong leader and a worthy Alpha, until the end."

My chest tightened as the casket was lowered into the earth. The man had taken me into his pack and given me a home with Rachel. Cared for me, defended me from the judgment of others...

He was gone.

There was a part of me that still couldn't believe it.

Despite my own sorrow, I needed to stay strong for Allara. She leaned close, pressing into my side as she watched the soil being poured into the grave.

The pack was silent, watchful. The only sound was the wind whistling through the clearing.

The branches above us whispered and stirred, like the trees were passing secrets amongst themselves.

A loud thud startled me. After a moment, I realized it was Elder Mason's staff slamming into the ground. All eyes turned to him.

He gave a creaking cough before he started to speak.

"The time has come for us to announce a new Alpha," he said. His voice reminded me of the rustle of dry, papery leaves. "An Alpha to emerge from the ashes and replace our fallen leader. An Alpha to carry us forward, into a new era for the pack."

I inclined my head so that I could whisper to Allara without being overheard by those next to us.

"I don't think I've ever heard Elder Mason speak publicly before."

"Neither have I," she murmured. "But, shh!"

"My council has consulted upon this matter for several moons now, leading up to this day. The previous Alpha guided us in our decision and offered his blessing. Though some among you may doubt it, I believe that our new leader will prove worthy of the responsibility."

I glanced across at Jaime, who was whispering something to Jason. Jaime's eyes were glittering and his face was pale. His gaze was fixed on Allara, who was too absorbed by the Elder's words to notice.

My hackles rose. My wolf sensed danger.

I slid my arm around Allara's waist, resisting the urge to shield her with my body.

"The role of Alpha shall pass through the true bloodline," Elder Mason announced, and a ripple of surprised noise rolled through the crowd.

Hang on a second...

True bloodline?

But... that means...

"Allara Bane." The Elder turned to her, and held out the thick, dog-eared tome he was carrying in front of him. "Do you accept responsibility for the pack of your father, and his father before him?"

Cold with shock, I could do nothing but stare down at Allara.

Her lips were parted and shock was reflected in her expression. Frozen to the spot, she blinked up at me, and then back to Elder Mason, in turn.

I gave her a gentle nudge.

"I... ah..." She reached out and touched the ancient record book, tracing her fingertips over the tome's binding. "I... do. I accept."

She cleared her throat and raised her chin. "I accept," she repeated, louder and firmer this time.

I spared a glance over to the other side of the circle, where Jaime stood with his fists clenched. His face was almost incandescent with fierce emotion.

"Very well." The Elder inclined his head in somber acknowledgement. With slow, reverent movements, he opened the book and drew a small silver knife out of his pocket, laying it down on the page in front of him with the handle pointed toward her.

On the left-hand side, I could see the name of Allara's father recorded in dark red, and his signature and seal, a little faded around the edges.

The right side page was blank, ready and waiting for the next Alpha's mark.

"*No!*"

A piercing cry came from the other side of the circle, traveling over the freshly settled earth of the grave mound. It was Jaime.

Allara paused, her hand outstretched to take the knife.

"Allara." I put my hand on her arm and tried to hold back the rumbling growl that threatened to take over my voice. "Ignore him. Sign the book."

Jaime called out again, his voice echoing through the clearing. Two men jumped forward to restrain him, but even so, his fury was so intense they only just managed to hold him back and prevent him from shifting into wolf form.

His eyes flashed silver, full of disbelief and rage.

"Allara Bane," he shouted. "I challenge you."

Everyone froze to their spot.

He had said the one thing we couldn't ignore.

The one thing that was bound to catch the attention of every single pack member, right down to the smallest child.

"Tomorrow," he spat, shaking himself free of the men restraining him. "We battle. You and me. Whoever wins becomes Alpha."

Jaime stood with his back straight and regarded Allara with a look of visceral hatred.

I let out a growl, unable to hold it in any longer; it was like a switch flipped as I took in his aggressive body language. His stance was enough to trigger my instinctive fight response. If he shifted into his wolf form now, I would be sure to follow, and I couldn't guarantee there would anything left of Jaime for Allara to fight.

I took deep breaths, trying to control myself. I had to let this play out the correct way. The pack had to see Allara step up and take control. It was the only way for her to prove her leadership qualities.

But I didn't have to like it.

"And whoever loses?" she called. Her voice rang out loud and clear, so that everyone could hear.

The way she spoke reminded me of our fight at her condo. The one that brought her here.

It was only a couple of days ago, but it felt like a lifetime.

"Oh, didn't I mention?" Jaime gave her a smirk. He was savoring this moment; I could tell. Making assumptions about his own strength, and her weakness. "We fight to the death."

My stomach dropped out from under me.

No.

"No, no, no!"

It took a moment to realize I'd shouted the words out loud, because Allara tugged on my wrist.

"I got this," she muttered, before raising her voice so that it could be heard all the way across the clearing. "I *am* the Alpha, Jaime. It's in my blood. My lineage. It was always going to be this way!"

"Then *prove it!*" he yelled back. Even from this distance, I could see the way his body still trembled with suppressed rage. To me, he looked to be on the edge of lunacy. The most dangerous kind of shifter to fight.

"What kind of Alpha abandons their own pack?" Jaime jeered. He pointed to her as he turned to address the crowd of funeral onlookers. "Her father's dead, and now she wants to stroll in and take charge. She ran out on us five years ago. She doesn't care about us. She left, and she'd do it again in a heartbeat!"

Allara sucked in a breath. "That's not—"

"You would allow a *woman* to lead you?" Jaime cut across her, before barkingd out a harsh laugh. "The Alpha named me successor years ago. Just because he changed his mind in the end, means nothing. He was right not to trust her. Why should you? She ran off. She betrayed her own kin!"

Murmurs rippled through the crowd. Nobody seemed convinced by Jaime, but nobody was shutting him down, either.

Some of the people around us looked skeptical, but most just looked afraid.

"She's hiding behind that *mongrel*." Jaime pointed at me, and I bared my teeth at him. "Like he'll save her. Look at her! She's barely even a wolf anymore, she's been away from us for so long. Who would respect a pack whose Alpha has forgotten who she is?"

My pulse raced, and my body trembled. It wouldn't be long before I shifted. Jaime's words were stirring up every protective instinct I had, and every cell in my body wanted to tear his throat out, right where he stood.

Allara's hand gave mine a final, warning squeeze before she stepped forward. Her head was high. Her dark hair flowed down her back like a river, looking almost blue in the places it caught the light from above.

Jaime is wrong.

She is the Alpha.

The light in her eyes was unmistakable. She was proud, unbending, regal.

All the years she'd been away from us fell away like water. They didn't matter; she wasn't changed. She had never belonged to the city, and it hadn't left an indelible mark on her. Her experiences there had shaped her, yes. But she was still Allara.

Still a wolf.

More of a wolf than ever, in fact.

"I accept," she shouted, and my heart dropped. "I will meet your challenge for Alpha, Jaime, and I will win!"

"What are you doing?" I hissed, horror flooding my senses, even though I knew she had to do this.

My actions had ensured that she had no choice.

By bringing her back here, I had put her in this position, where she had to fight him.

After so long, I'd finally gotten her back, only to risk losing her again. This time, for good. I had led her into enormous danger. She would have been safer remaining in the city.

I'd just signed the death warrant of the woman I loved.

"You have to trust me," she whispered. She stared at me, and her blue eyes were filled with resolve.

"I do," I said, brushing my fingers lightly over her cheek. "I *do*."

And I did trust her, more than anyone. I trusted in her loyalty and integrity, and her determination to do the right thing, no matter the cost to herself.

But I knew that the man standing on the other side of the clearing didn't care about trust, or honor.

I knew that, whatever happened tomorrow, he wasn't planning on playing fair.

Jaime met my gaze and smirked, his eyes glittering. He had the taste of victory already on his tongue.

THE PACK WALKED BACK through the forest, past the meeting house. I kept Allara separate from the clusters of pack members who stared at us unashamedly as she passed, walking so that my body sheltered hers from their gaze.

It was the least I could do for her.

Helpless fury burned its way right to my core. She had been placed in an impossible situation. One that I had inadvertently created. If I hadn't meddled with her fate, Jaime would be Alpha right now, and she would be safe and sound in the city, none the wiser.

In the back of my mind, I knew the situation wasn't that simple. The pack would have been screwed, either way. With Allara, at least they had a shot.

And her father had needed to see her, before the end.

But damn it.

Now *she* was in danger, and there was nothing I could do to protect her.

I managed to keep my thoughts to myself, all the way back to the house. Once the front door shut behind us, I couldn't bring myself to hold it in any longer.

The tension had been steadily mounting between us as we walked. Now, I let it spill out into the open air.

"Don't do this."

Through some effort, I managed to keep my voice steady. She had her back to me.

She became still, the line of her shoulders rigid with tension.

"You're putting yourself in danger," I continued. "Jaime... this is what he wants. You're a threat to him, Allara. He'll *destroy* you."

She didn't turn. Instead, she walked away, disappearing through the archway of the kitchen. I followed her, only to find her staring out of the window into the forest, with a pensive expression.

"Allara." I placed my hand on her shoulder, taking care not to startle her or show too much of the panic I felt. "There's still time. You can take it back, you *can*. Just go to him and tell him you won't do it."

She twisted out of my grasp and fixed me with a glare strong enough to knock the wind out of me.

"Take it *back*? Are you serious?"

"Yeah!" Recovering, I threw out my hands defensively. "Screw Jaime!"

She just stared at me, saying nothing.

After a moment, all the pent-up frustration drained out of my body. I was exhausted. I ruffled the hair on the back of my head with one hand, sighing.

Once Allara set her mind to something, there was nothing anyone could say to put her off her course.

To tell the truth, it was one of the things I loved most about her.

Usually.

I huffed out a long breath and sat down at the small table by the window. I had to choose my next words carefully.

"Your dad wouldn't have wanted this, you know that," I said, softly. "He'd want you to be safe."

She made a noise of irritation and slumped into the chair opposite me. She hid her face in her hands, her hair tumbling forward and obscuring her expression.

"I don't have a choice, Reid," she mumbled, so quietly I almost missed it. "You know I don't."

I thought fast.

"We'll leave together, while we still have the chance." I drummed my fingers against the table and pulled up a mental map, plotting our route in my head. "The truck's got enough fuel to get us at least as far as Bridgeport. We can hop around, stay in motels... maybe head for the east coast. See those beaches you love so much."

I smiled wistfully.

Before she could say anything, I continued. "Or up north, far north. Somewhere remote, where no-one will come looking for us. I can pick up work along the way... You wouldn't have to worry about anything, I swear. We'll find a place, Allara. I'll keep you safe."

She looked up at me, her eyes wide. "You... you really mean all that, don't you?"

I bit my lip, dropping my gaze. "Yeah. I really do. We gotta get far away from here, and we gotta go now."

She stared at me as if in disbelief. Then she reached out and took my hand, drawing it closer to her. I wound my fingers through her hair and pulled her forward, kissing her forehead.

She squeezed my hand tight, and then let it go.

"I can't leave," she said, after a long moment.

I growled my frustration. "He'll hurt you, Allara! He'll *kill* you. And he'll enjoy it while he does that."

"You said you trust me."

Her accusation hurt. "I do trust you. But I don't trust him. He won't play fair, Allara. He'll use every dirty trick in his arsenal. He wants you *dead*."

"I know." She traced a pattern on the tabletop. "But he'll hurt the entire pack if he becomes Alpha. He's crazy, Reid. I saw that, today. So, I can't abandon everyone. Not again…" She stared past me, out of the window at the forest beyond. "He's right, you know. I did leave everyone behind. If I leave now, why did I come back at all? Why did *you* bring me back?"

Her head snapped back to face me; her gaze was sharp and unrelenting.

Maybe it was always going to play out like this. Allara wouldn't walk away from people who needed her. It wasn't in her nature.

And right now, our pack needed her. Whether they knew it or not, she was the only one who could protect them from Jaime.

If she survived tomorrow.

Jesus. Why *had* I brought her back here?

So she could see her dad one last time.

Because she's the only thing standing in the way of Jaime wreaking havoc across the entire state.

Shit, I couldn't lie anymore. Even to myself.

Not now that she was finally back in my arms. No longer a memory, but flesh and blood. Real.

I'd brought her back because *I* needed her. Plain and simple.

My thoughts were interrupted when she gave a heavy sigh.

"If I refuse his challenge, and take over as Alpha anyway…" She paused, lost in thought. "They'll never accept me. You know that, Reid."

I knew. I also didn't need to ask who she meant by 'they'. The council, the pack elders. Hell, everyone in our community. She was right.

Elder Mason had proclaimed her the rightful successor to her father. She could sign her name in that book in her own blood, perform all the rites, and be declared Alpha.

But none of that would mean Jaime's challenge would be forgotten.

She couldn't step into the Alpha role having turned her back on a rightful challenger on her very first day leader. It would be an unforgivable display of weakness, and it went against every code of law followed by our kind.

Then there was Jaime himself.

He had Allara in his sights. Like any vicious predator, he wasn't about to let her get away without a fight.

Even if we left the pack, we would never be truly free of him. He would cast a shadow that would find us, wherever we went.

He wanted to snuff her out.

The realization filled me with dismay, and I couldn't stop myself from pressing my point.

"There's got to be another way," I said. "This isn't a gamble you have to take, Allara."

"Yes, it is."

She stood up. The late afternoon sun shone through the window and she lingered in the light for a moment, bathed by it. The loose strands of her hair glowed, framing her face like a halo.

She had always taken my breath away.

"I've already made up my mind," she said. Her eyes glimmered as she looked at me.

I was transfixed, unable to look away.

"You *know* that. I'm done running away from my fate. It's time to face it, Reid."

In that moment, I could truly see the Alpha she had already become. Her eyes held their own silvery light, like she was on fire from within.

"You should leave." Her hand slid down my arm, her touch cool and reassuring. "If he wins tomorrow..."

She trailed off. She didn't need to finish her sentence.

If Allara lost the battle, the next person Jaime would come after was her vengeful, grieving mate. *Me.*

Her unspoken statement filled me with surprise. Even now, after all this time, she didn't know.

Where you go, I go.

"I'm not going anywhere." In a couple of strides, I rounded the table and was by her side. I cupped her face in my hands and gazed into those sunlit eyes, then softly kissed the corner of her mouth. "I'm with you. Every minute."

She made a small noise and turned her head, drawing me closer for a deep, toe-curling kiss.

And I knew, in that moment, she did understand what she meant to me.

We understood each other perfectly.

ALLARA

I stared up at Reid, hardly daring to believe that we were back in this space, where anything was possible. Where we might get our second chance.

His hands were warm on my face. The look he gave me was blazing, and it heated me right down to my toes.

I turned my head to the side slightly, sliding my own hand up to cover his, and kissed his palm gently.

"Let's get out of here," he breathed. I raised an eyebrow at that, and he said, "Just for a little while. Not for good."

A grin spread across my face as I caught on to his meaning. Our special place.

My wolf surged up, ready to spring free.

With a seductive smile, I slipped out of his arms and padded over to the kitchen's back door. I opened it and stepped with bare feet out into the sunlight.

Hanging on to the doorframe, I cocked my eyebrow challengingly. "Race you?"

For a second, he stood there in the kitchen and stared at me, like he couldn't believe his eyes. After a moment, his brows lowered and his expression darkened, and a new kind of hunger crept into his gaze.

It was enough to make my cheeks heat, and a flush creep up from my neck.

Without warning, he gave a playful growl and sprang after me.

There were times when his wolfish qualities came right to the forefront, even in human form. He had always struck me as particularly wild, even compared to others of our kind.

His untamed qualities made my pulse race and called to the shifter in me.

My heartbeat thrummed in my chest like a trapped bird as I began to run, darting through the trees, his footfalls echoing all around me.

As I ran, I pulled off my drab black dress and let it fall to the forest floor, before shaking my loose hair out over my shoulders. I panted as adrenaline began to flood through me.

This was freedom. And it had been so long since I'd tasted it.

I shifted into wolf form.

Unlike the other day, this time the change was as effortless as breathing. I could run on four legs much faster than two, and I leaped through the air with the sheer exhilaration of the chase.

In spite of everything, it was good to be back.

Home.

It seemed like an eternity since I'd felt the sun on my back like this, or had time to stop and listen to the sounds of nature around me.

For a wolf, city life could be overwhelming.

The first couple of months had been hell. Every car alarm, police siren, and drunken argument outside my bedroom window had startled me, and my finely tuned senses became so rattled I barely slept.

But I'd gotten used to it.

Eventually, I'd managed to put my memories of the woods—memories of this place— in the same deeply-buried box in my mind where I put everything else that hurt too much to think about.

As I ran, I heard a deer chewing the foliage half a mile away. Somewhere nearby, a woodpecker hammered on tree bark. There were distant voices echoing from the village. The wake for my dad was still winding down, most of the tribe having adjourned to the meeting house.

I was aware of Reid's presence somewhere just behind my right shoulder. He was catching up to me, and fast.

I had always been smaller and lither than him. Today I used that to my advantage, ducking under a fallen branch, weaving through tight spaces, and sprinting away before he could catch me. Our destination glimmered through the trees up ahead, and anticipation shot through me. I picked up my pace.

I burst through the tree line at the edge of the lake and dove in without hesitation.

The water was pleasantly cold, and I swam down into the depths, admiring the flickers of silver as fish darted through the dark reeds around me.

Reid crashed through the water after me.

His dive was markedly less graceful than mine. Any remaining fish in the area swam away in panic as shockwaves rippled through the water around us.

When I reached the surface and burst out into the sunshine, I realized I had transformed back into human once again.

The transition had been so seamless, so natural, that I hadn't even noticed.

I yelped with laughter when Reid followed me, emerging from

the depths still in wolf form, shaking out his fur and becoming a man again before my eyes.

He was grinning from ear to ear.

"Cheater," he laughed. "I would've won if you hadn't taken that shortcut!"

"If that's what you need to tell yourself." I splashed him playfully, and shrieked when he splashed me back. He grabbed me around the waist, dunking me underwater.

I squirmed away and resurfaced, gasping and spluttering with laughter.

His gaze was bright with unmasked joy. It raked over my torso, taking in the way my wet hair clung to my bare chest, accentuating my curves.

I grinned.

One track mind.

I could admit it, I wasn't much better. The way his water-slicked abs glistened in the sunlight made me want to do things to him.

Wonderful, unspeakable things.

It was amazing to think that, even though we had spent so many years together before being driven apart, my desire for Reid hadn't been quenched desire one bit.

If anything, our five-year separation had only intensified my need—because I remembered exactly what I'd missed.

I wanted to drink him in, have all of him. And this time, I never wanted to let him go.

I traced my eyes over his arms, his shoulders, appreciating the way his hair had slicked back in the water and the sunlight glistened off the hard planes of his body. He was still panting a little, from our race, and from something else.

Desire.

He made me greedy. I could drink and drink him in, take everything he gave me, and it would never, ever be enough.

In that moment, looking at the need etched on his face and then down to the hardening of his body beneath the clear water's surface, I knew that he wanted me just as much as I wanted him.

No more waiting...

He drew me toward him, pulling me through the water. His big hands settled around my hips. The movement was gentle, but firm with intent. I settled against him willingly and brought my arms up around his neck.

"You have no idea what you do to me," he murmured.

"Oh, but I do." I wiggled against him, and he groaned.

One hand came up to cup my breast and I bit my lip at the contact, releasing a moan. "When I'm around you..." His grin was crooked. "It's like I can't think straight."

I slid a hand into his hair and closed it into a fist, tilting his head back so I could bite lightly at his jaw and neck. "Oh, yeah?"

His breathing grew heavier when my lips moved farther down his chest. I could feel his heartbeat thudding against my mouth, and I smiled at the sensation, my tongue darting out to taste his skin.

"Reid." I looked up at him, meeting his lust-filled gaze. "At the diner. You asked me if... if I lived alone. I know what you meant. You wanted to know if... if there was anyone else."

A shadow fell over his face. His arms grew tense around me.

"I did."

My forehead dropped, resting against his chest.

"There's never been anyone else," I whispered. "I thought about it, once or twice, but I just couldn't. It felt wrong. There was only ever you."

His body trembled against mine. His arms gripped me tighter, hoisting me up, holding me close. I put my hands on his shoulders and let him carry me clumsily through the water to the shoreline.

He took me to the lake's edge and deposited me on the grassy bank.

Before, he'd seemed withdrawn, almost hesitant to touch me in the firm and confident way I remembered, after we'd kissed for the first time in five years. That night, he'd seemed content to let me take the lead.

He'd been holding back.

Now, there was no hesitation in the way he crawled between my legs and hooked my knees over his wide shoulders. His movements were quick and instinctive, and they brought me back to a different time.

In that moment, he reminded me of his teenage self, always ready to go in those brief stolen moments when we had the chance to slip away from everyone and be alone.

My head fell to the side and I arched my body up toward him, but his hand snaked over my hips, holding me still. He kissed the insides of my thighs until my toes curled and I grappled blindly for his hand, tangling his fingers with mine.

The sight of his head between my thighs sent an even stronger pulse of heat through me, and I stared up at the leaves above my head, dappled with golden light, wondering how I'd gotten so lucky to have this second chance at happiness.

He licked my flesh and sucked on my clit until I was writhing on the bank and crying out for him to come to me. I couldn't handle any more teasing.

I wanted him close. I wanted him inside me. I wanted to come around him, as he released his hot seed within me.

I grabbed a fistful of his hair and dragged him up my body, kissing him deeply. I moaned at the feeling of his firm chest pressing against mine and wrapped my arms around his torso, clinging to him shamelessly.

His lips brushed against the shell of my ear, and I writhed and bucked as he rocked his hips and thrust his cock into me.

"So gorgeous," he groaned into my neck, and I responded readily, wrapping my legs around his waist and driving his length impossibly deeper. "So beautiful. You're so…"

A wave of bliss bubbled up in my chest at the sound of his low voice, his need for me. I brushed back his hair, staring up into those incredible eyes, insensible with desire.

"Allara. I..." He shuddered. His hair escaped my fingers, falling across his face, and a shadow of silver rolled across his gaze. "I love you."

"I love you too," I managed, moments before he began to drive into me with hard purpose, over and over again.

Every other thought fell from my head so that all I felt was him. Inside of me. Over me. Possessing me. Consuming me.

Reid was my love. My mate.

My one true love.

And as we cried out together, reaching an ultimate climax at the same time, I knew I'd never be able to live without him again.

WE LAY on the bank at the edge of the lake until the light started to fade. Reid's eyelids were half closed and he seemed about ready to pass out, but I knew he was still alert to our surroundings.

If he'd been in wolf form, his ears would have flickered at the sound of every leaf rustling, every twig snapping. His fur would've been tufted up, standing on end.

I trailed my hand down his bare skin and goosebumps appeared where my fingers had been.

He groaned. One eye blinked open, staring at me. Gray eyes, fringed with dark lashes. No silver, now that he was sated.

They changed like the weather, Reid's eyes. When he was angry, they swirled like a storm, and they grew pale and still when he was sad, or deep in thought. Right now, they were calm. The color of woodsmoke.

I loved his eyes. I loved everything about him.

He grinned, flashing his white teeth at me, before flopping onto his back.

"You don't know what you do to me," he said. He whistled low through his teeth. "It's like, I have a plan. And then you come along, and everything flies off the rails. Been that way ever since we met, Allie."

"Oh, yeah?" Feeling bold, I pressed a kiss onto his shoulder, and then another. Slowly, my mouth trailed down his bicep. "Didn't know I was so distracting."

"Allara," he murmured, cupping the back of my neck and forcing me to meet his eye. His expression grew serious. "Five years ago…"

I tensed.

Way to ruin the moment.

"What?" My tone was carefully neutral.

"I… I made the wrong call. I shouldn't have listened to your father." He pressed his forehead against mine. "I was a stupid kid. The pack should never have come between us. I should have found a way for us to be together, no matter what."

"Yeah?" I breathed, hardly daring to believe that he was admitting such a thing.

His mouth met mine for one dizzying moment, and then he pulled back, his fingers twisting themselves through my hair.

"Forgive me. I didn't stand up for you. For us. I regret it every day."

He did?

I tried to hide the rush of emotion that flooded through me.

"You were obeying your Alpha," I said. "You had no choice."

"There's always a choice," Reid said simply. "And for me, it's always gonna be you."

My heart skipped. "Is that so?"

"Yes, ma'am."

His smile was wide and utterly, blindingly perfect.

I closed my eyes, and let myself believe I could have him like this forever, even though the promise of tomorrow wasn't a certainty.

CHAPTER 12

REID

We slept again at her dad's house that night, though sleep was a relative term, at least for me. I could barely sleep at all, no matter how hard I tried.

I lay with my arms around Allara, watching the dawn creep over the horizon outside and listening to the sounds of the birds rustling in the trees.

A hundred thoughts raced through my head.

I couldn't shake the constant, nagging fear that Allara would get hurt.

I wouldn't allow myself to contemplate the possibility that I might lose her.

For good this time.

I had one shred of hope on my side.

I knew that if Allara was facing death at Jaime's hands, I could step in and offer myself as her champion. I would face execution, and she would be safe.

It may not be her ideal outcome, but it was a hell of a lot better than the alternative.

She would never agree to the idea if I voiced it before the battle. In her mind, she needed to be the one to defeat Jaime's challenge, so the pack would accept her as their leader.

I understood the position she was in, but that did not mean I had to like it. Nor would I accept her death as any sort of outcome.

She mumbled a little in her sleep and my arms tightened around her body. She was so strong, so determined to do the right thing. But the fact remained that she was out of practice in her shifter form. As fast and smart as she was, Jaime had years of training under his belt, a mean streak a mile wide, and a point to prove.

And, if it came down to it, I would gladly go to my death protecting her.

To an outside observer, she would probably seem confident, even laid back.

I knew her better than that. When she was getting ready, her hands had trembled slightly as she wound her long hair into a braid, and she deliberated for too long over what to wear, pulling out every item she had brought back with her as well as everything she'd left behind, and laying it all on the bed.

She'd never been one for fancy dresses. Like me, she usually kept it simple: plain tees and worn-in jeans, with combat boots to top it all off. Perfect for hiking over rough forest terrain.

"What does it matter?" I said. "You're gonna be in wolf form, no-one will care what you wear beforehand."

She glanced at me, her brow furrowed. "It matters, okay? I can't go out there looking like the same old Allie! If I'm destined to be the *Alpha*, Reid, I have to look the part."

I put up my hands in a gesture of surrender. "Okay, okay! Your call."

"I have to go out there like... I already know who I am." She straightened her neck and rolled out her shoulders.

To me, it didn't matter what she wore. Being an Alpha was innate, not dependent on anything external. Allara was an Alpha in my eyes already.

In the end, she settled on a pair of calf length boots over her jeans and her favorite sweater. Her eyes landed on her old leather jacket, that had hung on the back of her bedroom door for as long as I could remember.

Her bedroom was exactly as she'd left it. Her dad hadn't moved a thing. I wasn't sure how Allara felt about that. When she first saw it, she had stopped in the doorway for a long time. A sheen of tears had brightened her eyes, but she hadn't said anything then.

"Reid?" she said now, bringing me out of my reverie. She walked over and took down the jacket, then brought it over to show me.

Up close, I realized that it was an old one of mine.

She had stolen it a lifetime ago.

I had long since grown out of it, but it fit her perfectly. The collar was crooked, and the elbows had been re-patched on countless occasions. It reminded me of happier times, when our only problems revolved around not getting busted for sneaking out into the woods at night.

She slipped on the jacket, adjusted her braid, and looked up at me. The image changed: suddenly, she wasn't the carefree teenager I'd once known.

She was a woman.

A strong Alpha.

She's mine, I thought, and quelled my inner wolf before it could emerge. It wasn't the time, or the place to claim her.

Up until then, I hadn't realized how detached from the pack she'd been when she traveled back to us in her city garb. How uncomfortable she had seemed in her stiff funeral attire.

Now, it truly felt like she was a part of the pack again. The battered leather jacket, with its clinking hardware, was all the battle armor she needed.

"What do you think?" She fixed me with a challenging stare, her mouth lifting at the corners.

"Perfect," I said. "Ready?"

She nodded. "Let's do this."

∼

As Jaime had been Allara's challenger, he was the one to choose the arena for the fight.

He had selected a clearing about a mile away from the village, surrounded by overhanging trees on one side and a rocky outcrop that tumbled into the ravine below on the other.

I did my best to hide my irritation.

Leave it to Jaime to go all dramatic.

He was a showman of the worst kind, and he clearly wanted to give the pack something to remember.

He wanted to defeat the last symbol of the old bloodline. He wanted to be the victor of a story that would be told around endless campfires for years to come.

The whole pack gathered at the edge of the tree line, ready to watch the action.

I couldn't see Allara anymore; she had greeted everyone with a quiet confidence when we first arrived, and then wandered off, presumably to prepare herself mentally for what was about to happen.

There were some ancient, uprooted trees that served as benches, and a few hollows in the rockface that the elders settled in, whispering amongst themselves. On closer inspection I realized that these carved-out spaces were manmade.

Somebody had taken the time to make seats, like this place had been used for gatherings before.

Battles, I guessed. Or... rituals. I traced my fingers over the grooves in the rockface, and the back of my neck prickled with anxiety.

There was a light touch on my shoulder, accompanied by a soft, familiar voice.

"This place is famous," Rachel said. "Must have been used to settle hundreds of scores. It's been around since before Allara's grandfather's time."

I forced myself to appear relaxed. I turned and gave her an uneasy smile.

"Too showy for me," I said.

She chuckled and grabbed me into a hug. I hugged her back tightly and she whispered into my ear, her voice low and urgent.

"Allie needs you. Go to her." She pulled back and looked me over, reaching up to brush the shoulders of my jacket. "Whatever happens out there... you keep your cool, all right? Promise me, Reid."

I gazed down at her. Even though she barely came up to my chest, she always had a way of making me feel like the little kid who had shown up on the pack's doorstep with nothing but the clothes he stood in.

It was a lifetime ago now. But in so many ways, she was the only mother I had ever known.

Unable to meet her gaze, I glanced away. "You know I can't promise that. If she's in trouble..."

Out of the corner of my eye, I watched her expression fill up with sorrow. When she spoke, it was with understanding.

"I know." She rested her hand against my face, sighing. "You'd do anything for her. But I had to ask. I'm proud of you, Reid. Whatever happens, remember that."

I nodded. "Thank you, for everything, Rachel."

I walked away from her with a heavy weight in my chest, and made my way through the trees in the direction Rachel had pointed, until I came upon Allara.

She was sitting on a boulder, staring into space. She didn't seem to hear me approach, because when she looked up, her expression was startled.

I knelt in front of her and took her face in my hands, staring deeply into her eyes. "You got this," I said, more to reassure myself than her.

"Jaime has the edge." She hung her head. Her braid swung toward me, and I tugged on it lightly. "He's strong. He's ready for this."

"He's arrogant. He thinks he has this in the bag." I extended a hand, pulling her up. "You can use that arrogance; turn it against him. Plus, you're faster than him. You're *smarter*. Remember all of those things, Allie."

She nodded, but doubt still flickered in her eyes. My chest went cold.

She can't doubt herself. Not now.

I could fight on her behalf, but she could hold her own against Jaime, at least for a little while.

She had to.

"Reid." She smiled softly. "I—"

Before she could finish, a howl pierced through the forest. A flock of birds took off from a nearby tree, their wings beating at the undergrowth.

"I know." I kissed her forehead for a final time. "I know. Me too."

This was not the time to declare our love once again, or to wish that things might be different. She had to concentrate.

She nodded, lifted her chin, and stepped away from me.

Maintaining eye contact, she slipped off her leather jacket and laid it on a nearby log. Her sweater followed, then her boots and jeans.

Finally, she stood naked before me. Framed by greenery like this, she looked ethereal, like a goddess of the forest.

"I believe in you, Alpha," I said, and in that moment, hope filled me.

She could do this. She could save our pack.

Her eyes glimmered with silver, and my whole body tingled. I had to back away before I shifted into wolf form alongside her.

Not yet.

Not knowing entirely why, I picked up her jacket and hugged it against my chest.

She gave me one final, unreadable glance before she turned away, padding off into the trees. I followed her through the forest, back to the clearing where Jaime and the others waited.

I rubbed the old leather between my fingers. It was stupid, but I wanted something of hers to hold onto while I was forced to watch...

No. Don't even think it.

Allara would survive.

I trusted her, and I trusted myself to back her.

I would do whatever it took to ensure that she survived this.

The alternative was unthinkable.

Rachel stood at the edge of the gathering. As I approached, she beckoned me to her side.

My gaze wandered over to the group of elders. Jaime's father Terry sat among them, looking as stoic as ever. He met my eyes and gave me a brief nod of acknowledgment.

Although he shared his son's fair hair, that was where the resemblance ended.

As far as I knew, Terry had always been faithful and supportive, the ideal second-in-command for Allara's father. He had never treated me with the disdain that some of the pack members showed, and he could usually rein in Jaime's more fiery impulses.

Usually.

I wondered if he knew what his son had in store for the pack, if he won today.

Did he know the extent of his own flesh and blood's craziness?

Before I could contemplate any further, a vicious growl erupted from the other end of the clearing.

Jaime.

I bristled with tension. If I had been in wolf form, my fur would have been standing on end at the sight of him.

Allara, in wolf form, loped into the clearing with her head held high, circling wide so that she could acknowledge the crowd of spectators up close. She looked regal; her carriage remained unbowed, as was befitting a wolf of her status.

Jaime dragged up the earth, raking it with his claws. His growl built until it seemed to shake the ground beneath our feet.

He was trying to rile her up, bait her into attacking first.

She appeared to pay no attention to him. One of her ears flicked back and forth, like she was trying to swat away an annoying fly.

Finally, she turned to her opponent.

Silence fell as they faced each other down. From where I was sitting on a fallen log next to Rachel, I could see Jaime's flank rising and falling rapidly. The muscles in his back legs were coiled with tension.

Although he was bigger than her, he was slighter than most of the male wolves in the pack. He had a wiry, deadly strength, and a reputation for using it with an unbridled savagery; a chunk was missing from his left ear, and even from a distance I could see his muzzle was heavily scarred.

He was glowering at Allara, practically frothing with bloodlust.

My fingers dug into the bark of the log, anchoring me in place.

I have to let her do this.

Without warning, he leapt for her.

His jaws were already wide, preparing to close around her throat.

He'll snap her neck in an instant. It'll be over before it has begun.

Moving impossibly fast, she met him halfway. They clashed in mid-air, their two bodies crashing down to earth in a blur of claws, fur, and teeth.

Snarls and growls filled the previous silent arena.

In a flash, I was transported back to our fight in Allara's backyard, before we left the city.

It had been a close call, too close for my liking. Both of us had pushed to the edge of our strength and dexterity. But that battle had been completely different to this one.

Death had never been the chosen outcome for either of us.

Our battle's undercurrent had held a different kind of intensity. Our passion for each other had been obvious, even then; we wanted to draw each other as close as possible, taste the other's delicious scent while we had the chance.

This was... different.

The fight between Jaime and Allara was vicious, frantic, and merciless. They were both going for the kill, snapping at each other's jaws with an impossible speed and ferocity. If either one reached the other's neck, it would likely be over in an instant.

Jaime had the size advantage, and he used it. He kept pressing forward, forcing Allara back onto the defensive. I watched with bated breath as he manage to close his teeth around her back leg, but she shook free and slid out from under him before he could fully bite down.

Although she was giving it everything she had, I could tell Allara was flagging. She kept feinting to the left, and I realized she was trying to draw Jaime away from the crowd of watching pack members.

I growled in frustration.

Allara. She was too busy thinking about danger to others, when she should be focusing fully on her own peril.

Typical.

Jaime lunged again. His bite didn't manage to gain purchase, but he did tear at Allara's ear. She whined, blood dripping down from her wound and soaking the earth between them.

Jaime loped back a few paces. His movements were unconcerned and almost lazy. He was enjoying this, taking his time.

Arrogance. There it was. *Use it against him,* I willed her.

Rachel placed her hand on my arm. I realized that my fists were clenched, and my knuckles were white. I forced myself to relax my muscles and concentrated on slowing my ragged breathing.

In, out.

Allara backed up, drawing Jaime farther away from the tree line.

In, out.

He lunged at her again, crowding over her until she bore down into the earth. He was forcing her to lie flat to protect her stomach. Her ears were peeled back, and her eyes were wide and fearful.

She was showing her fear? That wasn't good.

In, out.

Jaime's jaws closed around the scruff of her coat. Too close. Far too close to her neck.

He dragged her to her feet and shook her violently between his teeth.

I couldn't stand it any longer. I had to help her.

Shaking Rachel's hand off my arm, I felt the air around me grow hazy and distorted. Adrenaline raced through me, and my heart beat a mile a minute.

Jaime dropped Allara into the dirt and nudged at her with his paw like he was playing with his prey. Though they were some distance away by now, I could see her chest rising and falling rapidly.

"Allara!" I bellowed, dropping with a thud onto my knees.

I was dimly aware of Rachel and a couple of others pulling at my chest, holding me back. They were trying to stop me from shifting. I gritted my teeth, heeding their warning, but ready to throw them off if I had to.

Jaime held Allara down, right at the very edge of the outcrop. One wrong move and he would send her tumbling over the edge onto the jagged rocks below.

Allara give a soft whimper. Though my blood still raced, and I felt like I was about to explode, the noise caused a memory to flicker in the back of my mind.

Allara doesn't sound like that.

Although panic was flooding my body, I held my breath for a few seconds and thought about that noise.

I'd sparred with her hundreds of times. When we were mad at

each other, when we wanted to solve an argument, when we were happy, sad, bored, or for any reason at all.

I had never heard her make that whimpering sound before.

Except... once.

It had been years ago, when we were teenagers who would skip out on long and boring pack meetings to go spar in the forest for hours.

I scrambled to my feet after shifting back to human form, and kicked moodily at the dust, glaring at nothing in particular while Allara picked up a blanket and wrapped herself in it, laughing and laughing.

"You look so mad!" she said, delight in her tone.

"Yeah," I said, feeling belligerent. "You tricked me!"

"I did not!"

"Did too!" I snagged my jeans and tugged them up quickly. The conversation would be much more embarrassing if we both remained naked. "You pretended you were scared. Made me hesitate. I would've pinned you otherwise."

"Well..." She chuckled at the look on my face. "It worked, didn't it?"

I grumbled and took her hand, pulling her close to me. "I won't be such an idiot next time."

"Maybe you won't underestimate me next time." She flicked my ear with the tip of her finger, and I couldn't help but grin at her. I threw my arm around her shoulders as we headed back through the woods to the village.

My vision cleared.

Jaime wasn't toying with Allara.

Allara was toying with *Jaime.*

She was doing exactly as she should, taking advantage of his arrogance; his cocksure bravado. She knew he wanted to put on a big show for the pack and take out his competition in a public show of dominance.

She knew he would assume his victory was set in stone the moment she appeared to back down.

Even though I was focused on what was happening here and now, part of me reconsidered our fight, back in the city.

Had that gone her way as well?

I thought about what had happened after I pinned her. Maybe, after all that... she had wanted my win just as much as I did.

Maybe she'd *wanted* to come home, but had been too stubborn to admit it out loud.

Lightness filled my heart. She wanted to come back. With me.

Then I narrowed my eyes, studying them. Nothing was guaranteed. She was still in a great deal of danger.

After all, it wasn't over yet.

I calmed down enough that I wasn't about to shift into wolf form, but the sight of Allara so close to the edge of that precipice still had me on the verge of panic.

She told me to trust her.

And I did, down to my bones.

Jaime still had Allara pinned to the ground. One paw rested on her chest, almost like he couldn't be bothered to fully restrain her. His ears pricked up and he looked out over the pack, surveying the scene.

Letting everyone drink in his superiority.

The Alpha's daughter... defeated. About to be silenced forever, along with any memory of her father's legacy.

In a move so quick that everyone watching let out a collective gasp, Allara twisted out from beneath his restraining paw, and sprang up. The move swept Jaime's front legs out from under him, and he yelped, obviously shocked.

He staggered for a moment, caught off balance, before falling sideways and scrabbling. He couldn't seem to get purchase, and slid backwards towards the rocky edge of the ravine.

Before he had a chance to fall, Allara pinned his forelocks to the ground, holding him firmly in place.

Making sure he didn't fall to his death, I realized. As, indeed, did everyone watching.

Silence fell over the pack.

Then, into the silence, Allara threw back her head and howled.

The sound reverberated through the forest, sending shockwaves down my spine. The faces of the people around me were tight with tension.

The only figure of calm was Elder Mason, who stood near the center of the gathered crowd, surveying the scene with his cloudy, half-blind gaze.

"It is as decreed," he declared in his strange voice. He glided to the front of the crowd, his walking stick hitting the ground with a resounding *thud* at every step. "The Alpha's daughter shall take her place as the rightful heir."

A shiver went through the pack as they processed the outcome of the fight. Then, moving as one, every member of the council lowered their gaze to the earth and raised their right hand, placing it over their heart.

"Allara Bane!" they cried, and their hands flew upwards as if they were offering her name to the sky.

Thud. Thud. The wooden staff struck the ground.

It was done.

Allara was the new Alpha.

Her name echoed through the trees once more as the pack declared her their rightful leader.

I rushed forward, wanting to reach her, but Rachel put out a hand, stopping me in my tracks.

"Wait."

I turned toward her with a small growl. I had waited long enough.

What now?

CHAPTER 13
REID

But Rachel simply placed a woven blanket in my arms and gave me a gentle push.

"Go to her."

I gave her an apologetic smile and mumbled my thanks. I was grateful for her foresight, even if every cell in my body screamed at me to go to Allara *right this second*.

I held up the blanket. "You brought this for her. You knew she'd win?"

"I had a hunch." She patted me on the arm, smiling fondly. "Now go."

On impulse, I grabbed up Allara's leather jacket off the ground from where I'd dropped it, before I strode into the clearing, unable to stop myself from jogging the last few feet until I reached her crouching form. She had morphed back to human again, and was naked.

She had her back to me, and even from my angle of approach I could tell that she was panting harshly.

"Allara." She didn't seem to hear me. "Allara," I repeated, keeping my voice as soothing as possible. "I'm here."

Her head turned then, but just barely. If she were in wolf form, her ears would likely be twitching back and forth.

Moving slowly, I draped the blanket over her shoulders, covering her bare skin. After a moment her fingers came up, and she drew the blanket around her, wrapping herself in it.

She stood then, revealing her fallen adversary. Jaime lay sprawled out at her feet, staring up at her with an expression of hatred. The elder had decreed Allara the winner. There was no way for Jaime to win the fight now, even if he cheated and took her out after the fact, while in human form.

He would be shunned by the whole pack, and I would kill him.

Allara arranged the blanket so that it sat evenly over her shoulders. Her graceful movements made it seem like she wore a coronation gown rather than an old woolen blanket.

"The pack have declared it," I said in a low voice. "Once and for all. You are their Alpha, Allara."

Finally, she looked up at me. Her blue eyes were shining. She had never looked more beautiful.

"Don't I always tell you to trust me?" she said, granting me a soft smile.

I chuckled. "Maybe I should start listening."

She moved closer to me and pushed her forehead against mine, sighing. The sun glowed through the trees, and the wind flooded my senses with her gorgeous scent. It was a perfect moment.

Well, it would have been, except...

I pulled away and ran a thumb over her temple, snarling when I found blood there. "He hurt you."

Her face turned grave, and she glanced down at the silent figure lying at our feet.

"It looks worse than it is," she said, reaching up to touch the side of her head gingerly. "Reid... this isn't your fight."

"Your fight *is* my fight," I said simply.

Jaime sneered at me and his eyes glimmered with a hint of silver. I had to look away before I did something stupid.

Allara tugged at the jacket I held in my hands, distracting me.

"You brought my jacket," she said, giggling.

It *was* kind of silly, given the situation. But it felt right for her to have it while she faced the pack for the first time as their leader.

Careful not to jostle her, I lay the jacket loosely over the top of the blanket and brushed stray strands of hair away from her face with my fingers.

Now that my heart had stopped racing, I noted every scratch and bruise on her skin. They were scattered all over her face and jawline, and trailed over her collarbones and the exposed portion of her chest. My gaze drifted down to the monster at her feet.

"Reid," she said firmly. My eyes snapped back up to meet hers. "It's my call."

I inclined my head. "Yes, *Alpha*."

The heat of my gaze contrasted with my deferent tone, but I couldn't bring myself to change it.

If I were in her position, I would kill Jaime without remorse.

He had done enough damage—to us *and* to the pack, and if he had his way, he would do even more, destroying anyone who dared to stand in his way.

It wouldn't take much. He'd shifted back to human now and was already at the edge of the cliff, the perfect picture of submission. One push, and he would be out of our lives forever.

Allara seemed to be mulling over the same thought. She stared up at the sky and closed her eyes, standing perfectly still for what felt like an eternity.

Then, she opened them.

"No." She turned to me, and I knew her mind was made up. "Jaime lives."

I shook my head, readying myself to challenge her with everything I had. "It was a fight to the death. You have to do this."

"I won't." She stumbled a little and pressed her hand against her side, groaning.

I darted forward to catch her, but she refused to let me take her weight. *So stubborn.*

"I can't let bloodshed be my first act as the Alpha of our pack, Reid."

"Allara—"

"I knew it," Jaime spat. "She hasn't got the *stomach* for it. Just like her dear old Dad."

He sat back on his elbows and glared up at us. My blood was boiling, but I knew what the outcome of the fight meant for him. Some considered it a fate worse than death to be defeated. Humiliated in front of everyone.

Voices murmured behind us, and I looked up to find that the rest of the pack had come closer. They stood in a crowd a few paces away, watching and waiting.

"James Fletcher." Allara raised her voice so that everyone could hear. "As victor, I decide your punishment." She looked down at him, her demeanor cold and regal. "I will not kill you. Instead, I banish you from this pack. From this day until your last, you may never return here. When you die, your bones will not be laid to rest with those of your ancestors."

I spared a glance at the pack, wondering what they made of all this. Were they relieved by the outcome of the battle, or enraged?

I couldn't really tell. Only Terry's face stood out to me; the man looked white as a sheet.

A long silence followed Allara's words.

Slowly, Jaime got to his feet, grunting with pain. I felt a shadow of satisfaction that Allara had managed to give as good as she got. For someone so out of practice in her wolf form, she'd really done a number on him.

He straightened up, looking her right in the face. No deference to her status showed at all. His eyes were like ice.

"You'll regret your weakness," he said in a low voice that trembled with rage. "Someday soon. I promise you. You and your mongrel mate."

A growl built in my throat. Allara linked her arm through mine, pulling me away from Jaime until he stood alone at the edge of the cliff.

"Leave it," she murmured. "He knows it's over."

Without breaking eye contact, Jaime circled around us and backed away, his hands in the air in a mocking show of innocence.

Once he reached the edge of the clearing, he stopped and turned back, shouting,

"When the time comes and you're all sick of this little girl and her mutt, don't worry. I'll be there to take her place. She turned her back on you, but I never will!"

Without waiting for a response, he loped away, vanishing into the undergrowth.

I stared at the spot in the trees where he had disappeared, fighting the urge to follow and finish him. I knew that his threats weren't empty; this wasn't the last we would see of Jaime.

Allara's fingers threaded through mine, and I smiled as a new thought struck me.

We might have to watch our backs, but so would he. Allara was a force to be reckoned with. And she would have me by her side, from this time forward.

Casting my gaze over the crowd, I noticed that Jason was watching Allara with an unreadable expression. He glanced away when I caught his eye.

Kara murmured something in his ear, and he nodded.

Paul stood beside him, looking devastated. I told myself that it didn't mean anything. He'd just lost his best friend, after all.

Terry was a far bigger concern.

He stood a little apart from the others, staring out into the valley with a blank look on his face.

As the Beta of the pack's old leader, he would always have a place on the council, and the ear of the pack.

Not for the first time, I wondered whether he'd known about Jaime's plans. He'd always been a thoughtful man, the complete opposite of his hothead son.

Terry had counseled Allara's father for decades. I fervently hoped that he would understand the position she had been put in.

Then I understood the logic of sparing Jaime's life, as well as the compassion. The pack's new Alpha would have made a powerful enemy if she had killed Terry's son.

Rachel smiled at me, relief and hope in her eyes, and I smiled back. I owed her so much. I'd had nothing when she took me in...

Nothing worth holding onto, anyway.

"Looks like you got your wish, after all." Allara tugged on my hand, and I looked down at her.

"What's that?"

In spite of her tiredness and injuries, her face glowed. "You're stuck with me. I can hardly go back to the city now, can I?"

Acting on impulse, I picked her up and raised her off her feet. She squealed with surprise before laughing brightly.

"I'm sure we can find something for you to do here," I replied, burying my face in her hair and kissing her head before setting her down gently. "Alpha Bane."

She gave me a wicked grin. "At your service."

EPILOGUE

ALLARA

I sat in front of my dressing table mirror and peered at my reflection. I might just change that little strand...

Kara slapped at my hands as I tried to rearrange the wedding hairstyle that my friend had thoughtfully done for me. "Stop fiddling with it!"

I dropped my hands into my lap, trying to tamp down the guilt. *Oops. Busted.*

Time to put my trust in Kara.

She threw a smirk at my reflection via the mirror before continuing to weave her seemingly magic fingers through my hair. It was looped into a simple half-up, half-down style that looked simple and yet elegant.

As much as I loved what she'd done, my fingers itched to pull my hair free of its style, slip out of my fancy dress, and run far, far away.

I was about to get married, to the man I loved more than life itself, and I couldn't control my nerves.

Rachel appeared in the room, and I met her gaze in the mirror, smiling gratefully as she passed me a cup of herbal tea.

"Something to settle the nerves," she said.

"Do all brides feel like this?" It seemed ridiculous, to be stressed over something I actually wanted!

"Most do." Rachel patted my shoulder. "You'll have to get used to being stared at, Allara. You're the Alpha now."

I huffed a sigh. I knew that, of course. *But...*

"Everyone knows that Reid wasn't my father's first choice." Kara glanced at Rachel before resuming her fussing with my hair. "What if they all think I'm making a mistake?"

"But he's *your* choice." Rachel's hand on my shoulder squeezed gently. "It was always meant to be this way. In time, they'll come to understand that."

I prayed that Rachel was right about the others. I wanted them to accept Reid fully as one of us.

I hadn't lied to Reid when I told him there hadn't been anyone else. There had never been anyone else. I realized that now.

And I wanted to bond forever with my mate.

For me, and for Reid.

We'd been apart for so long. It seemed unthinkable now, that either of us had let the situation drag on. He had been following his Alpha's orders, at least, but I had been driven by hurt.

After we had picked up where we left off, the intervening years had melted away like a bad dream. I had a lot to be thankful for, and I couldn't wait to make my love for Reid official with the bonding ceremony.

But part of me knew that the mystery surrounding his origins would always leave people wondering, who was the man at the right hand of the Alpha?

Would he be my Beta wolf? My co-counsel? Would we lead the pack together?

They were only some of the questions that I didn't have the answers to, yet.

Finally, Kara finished fussing at my hair. I stood and straightened my skirt, turning to face her and Rachel. "Do I look okay?"

They nodded.

"More than okay. You look perfect." Rachel put a hand against my cheek. "You look so much like your mother."

"One finishing touch," Kara said. She picked up a simple circlet fitted with small amber stones, and reached up to drape it carefully over my head, so as not to disturb my hairdo. "There. *Now* you're good to go. You look awesome."

I don't feel like I'm good to go! I wanted to scream. *I feel like I'm about to melt into a puddle of tension.*

Nevertheless, I gathered my nerves together and made my way downstairs. Rachel helped me down the front steps of my house, and together we walked through the village, coming to a stop outside the meeting house.

"Just relax, take it one step at a time," Rachel said. "Remember, it's your day."

I felt some of the stiffness in my spine drain away as I climbed up to the entrance of the building.

Briefly, a wave of sadness hit, that my parents would not be here to see me wed Reid. But somehow, I felt their energy, their presence, and I knew that they would both be happy for me in this moment. I nodded, took a deep breath and released it, letting the sadness go. Then I entered the hall. As I did so, soft music began to play.

Elder Mason stood at the front on a raised dais that had been constructed for the occasion, holding a length of red velvet in his hands. The pack surrounded us on either side of the aisle. They stood patiently, about to witness the bonding of their Alpha to her mate.

Beside Elder Mason stood Reid.

As soon as I saw him, my tension melted away.

He was always the focus of my attention in whatever room he stood, but today I truly couldn't take my eyes off him.

He'd ditched his trusty leather jacket for the occasion, trading it in for a simple button down in a soft gray that fit his broad frame perfectly and made his eyes look even more striking. He had even tamed his hair somewhat, pushing it back so that I could see the strong line of his jaw as I approached.

He was everything I had ever wanted.

I came to a stop opposite him, meeting his gaze. The look on his face was hard to read, but there was a storm of emotion in his eyes.

You look beautiful, he mouthed.

My lips curved into a smile.

You too, I thought, and hoped he could read the appreciation in my gaze.

I'd never seen him so polished, though I'd always loved him best in flannel and his old boots.

Or naked… of course.

The music began to crescendo, swelling with intensity, and the drumbeat thundered around us, keeping time to the beat of my heart.

As one, we held out our right arms. Our wrists met in the empty space between us.

"The time has come," Elder Mason said, "for these souls to join together as one."

He held the velvet fabric up for those watching to see, and then wrapped it around our joined wrists, tying it once.

"Allara Bane," he continued. "You are bonded to Reid, body and soul, as the fates have foretold."

I inclined my head. The elder wrapped the cloth around us a second time, tying it again.

"Reid." His attention turned to Reid. "You are bonded to Allara Bane, body and soul, as the fates have foretold."

Reid bowed. Against the wrist that was now bound to his, one of his fingers brushed my arm gently.

"She is yours," Elder Mason said, magnifying his voice so that it filled the whole room. "And you are hers. As the fates have foretold!"

As one, the pack got to their feet, stamping on the floor and echoing his words in unison as a drumbeat started to play once more.

"As the fates have foretold!"

With his free hand, Reid pulled me forward by the waist and I melded into his body. He kissed me with a fierce intensity, our bound hands trapped between us.

When we broke apart, I flushed at the way we had displayed our passion for the whole pack to see.

I was faintly aware of applause, some scattered cheering, and a few wolf-whistles, but I pressed my forehead into Reid's and ignored it all, focusing only on him.

"Finally," he breathed, and then captured my lips for a brief, dizzying moment before pulling away and laughing softly to himself, like he couldn't believe it. "You're back. And you're *mine.*"

"As you are mine. Now, and always," I said simply.

We stood there, soaking in the moment. Then, Reid tugged at the ties that bonded us together.

"Do we have to keep these on forever?" he whispered, quirking an eyebrow. "Because I could work with that."

I chuckled, shaking my head.

"I think you're meant to untie us at some point. If you can figure out the knots," I added, winking.

Toward the back of the hall, I spotted my old boss Mick, Tammy, and Penny chatting to Kara and Jacob, and my heart skipped a beat or two.

I gave them a wave and a grin, and then tilted my head at Reid. "I didn't know they were coming!"

"I invited them. What?" he said. "City life can't have been all bad, right?"

With difficulty, given our current entanglement, I wrapped my arms around his neck and kissed his cheek. "I love you."

"I love you, too," he murmured, kissing my hair. His eyes were warm, and calmer than I'd seen them in a long time. "Always have. Always will."

~

THE FESTIVITIES WOUND on well into the evening. A long table was set up in the clearing, and lanterns were hung in the trees. Children ran back and forth, trying to catch the fireflies that glowed in the fading twilight.

Dancing began after the feast, and people spun around each other, skirts swirling, shouting with laughter. Reid was at the center of it all, playing ring-a-rosie with the smallest children and letting them clamber all over him as he chuckled.

I stood to one side and watched the people—*my* people—without really seeing them.

Too much stirred in my head to get completely lost in the joy of the moment.

I'm the Alpha now.

The thought shocked me still.

But my dream had come true.

Reid *had* stayed, just as he said he would. My duties weren't mine to carry alone.

Wherever you go, I go.

We had to protect everyone here from whatever lay out there, in the darkness beyond the trees. But we would do it, together.

"Most women look happier at their bonding ceremony," said a voice beside me.

I turned. Terry was holding a can of beer and studying me with interest.

"Don't fancy a dance with your new mate?"

I swallowed and shook my head, fiddling with the trailing edge of my sleeve. "Just tired, I guess."

The truth was, I did feel kind of weird. I had for a few days, now, but I'd chalked it up to bonding ceremony jitters.

"Hmm." He nodded. "The road ahead is long and winding, Allie. Better keep your strength up for what lies in front of you."

Before I could figure out what he meant, or formulate a reply, he drifted off, mingling with the revelers until I lost sight of him altogether.

What lies ahead?

Was he in contact with his son? What did he know?

My niggling worries could be paranoia on my part. Nevertheless, something made the hairs on the back of my neck stand up.

He was your dad's closest friend, I told myself.

So, we'd better keep an eye on him, replied another inner voice, which sounded remarkably like Reid.

I wonder what he'll do next...

Penny came bounding up to me, flushed with exertion from being spun around by the inhuman strength of dozens of wolf shifter men. "Hey, cheer up, sour face! It's your wedding! Or, close enough, right?"

"Right." I laughed, forcing a smile onto my face. "Having fun?"

"Tons." She grinned back at me. "Your hubby—or is it soulmate? Whatever. Reid's waiting for you! Go dance!"

At that, I shook off the niggle and grinned back at her. Penny was right; I could put away my Alpha responsibilities for just one night.

I wandered out onto the dance floor, where Reid waited for me. His eyes reflected the light of the flickering tapers around us, and his lips were stretch up into the most gorgeous smile I'd ever seen.

It might have taken a few bumps along the road to get here, but I knew now that we could take on whatever the future brought to our doorstep.

Because, finally, we were together.

AMELIA SHAW

THE END

~

Read on for a sneak peek of:

Love of the Wolf

Book 2 in the 'Pack Loyalty' series

~

CHAPTER 1

TAMMY

The forest outside flashed past my window in a blur as we drove.

I was sure the landscape was breathtaking this far outside the city, but I wasn't in the mood to take in any of the natural beauty that surrounded us. Up front, Mick and Penny were chatting —no, *gossiping*. Their topic of conversation was fixed on one thing: the mysterious stranger that Allara had eloped with a couple of weeks ago.

"I'm just saying, it's crazy she ran off with him like that!" Penny swiveled in her seat to catch my eye, and I gave her a half-hearted nod. This seemed to satisfy her because she turned back and continued her argument with Mick. "If any of my ex-boyfriends showed up like that, I wouldn't be taking them out on any diner dates, that's for sure."

I watched her long earrings swing from side to side as she talked. Penny was pretty, petite, and vivacious, a real firecracker. I wouldn't be surprised if she had to fend off a guy from time to time.

"Nah," Mick said. I could see his profile in the wing-mirror, and he was frowning. "I saw the way he looked at her. It was deeper than some past fling, I'll bet."

"Allara said he dumped *her,*" Penny mused. "What?" She laughed, catching Mick's raised eyebrow look. "So, I eavesdropped a little! It was past midnight and there were no other customers in the diner. You can't tell me you wouldn't have done the same."

Mick just harrumphed and caught my eye in the mirror. "Check the map, will ya? This place must really be out in the sticks."

Sighing to myself, I opened the map and spread it over my knees, running my finger over the route we had marked out.

Of all the road trips I'd taken, this one had to be the weirdest, for a few reasons.

Reason number one: the track we were on was narrow and winding, with steep banks cut into the rock on either side of us. It was completely unmarked on the map itself, so we were basically following a series of crosses Reid had drawn for us and praying we were on the right track. We were in remote territory now, and if we got lost, nobody had any bars of reception on their cell phones to call for help. I couldn't ask Allara for advice, even if we had reception. Reid had invited us as a surprise for her, so she didn't know we were coming.

Reason number two: Allara had disappeared, practically overnight. The only communication she'd left was a short note to Mick, saying she was fine and that she had to take care of some things at home, and she would only be gone for a few days. While this let us know that wherever she had gone, she was, hopefully, safe, it didn't give us much else.

Reason number three: the next thing that happened completely out of the blue was an invitation from her hunky guy Reid to their wedding in Allara's hometown. Out here somewhere, in the middle of nowhere.

Only he didn't call it a wedding. He'd called it a *bonding ceremony*.

I had to admit, this last bit intrigued me a little. I didn't have Allara pegged as the type to be into all that New Age, crystal healing stuff.

"Looks like we're on the right track," I said. "We passed that cave thing on the left a couple miles back, right?"

"I think so," Penny said, sounding uncertain.

She and Mick resumed their debating, and I tuned out, letting the sound of their voices wash over me as I went back to staring into space.

Truth be told, I hadn't known Allara very long. She was a good co-worker, and I loved working with her, but I'd always known the bar job was just a stop gap for her. A way to make ends meet, just like it was for me.

I was fresh out of college, having finally completed my last semester and gained enough credits to earn my degree in childcare. Allara and Mick had both surprised me by showing up to my graduation ceremony.

The one thing all my friends and family wanted to know was when I would start my training program to become a social worker. It had been my goal from the minute I'd started further education, and they all knew it.

I fobbed them all off and kept my answers vague and non-committal. There would be time for all that; and I was fine where I was. Mixing drinks wasn't exactly my idea of the best way to spend my weekends, but it paid the bills.

Besides, it wasn't like I had anyone to spend my weekends *with*.

Not anymore.

I shook off the dark thoughts and focused on Allara. This was going to be *her* day, after all.

I knew the other two were curious to see the mysterious bonding ceremony. Reid hadn't really described what would happen, but I got the sense that it wasn't like anything I'd seen before. Part of me knew I should be excited, too.

But I couldn't shake off my misery so easily. It had sunk its claws into me a month ago, and I knew it wasn't going away any time soon.

Time heals all things.

I wished I could believe it, but the advice I had heard from everyone around me felt empty and meaningless. I was alone, and the years stretched out ahead of me, barren as a desert.

No matter how I looked at the situation, the pain was still as deep as it had been since that night.

The night that had changed everything and turned my whole world upside down.

Nothing made sense anymore. I didn't know when things would turn right side up again, when the pieces of my life would fit back together like they did before.

In my heart of hearts, I suspected they never would.

It was midday by the time we rolled up the long narrow driveway.

There were trucks parked up against the banks of the road, mud coating their wheel guards. We hadn't seen any sign of life since we turned off the freeway, and it was a relief to see evidence of civilization this deep into the woods.

The trees were just like Allara had described the few times she'd talked about home. Their trunks were thick; some stood wider than our car's width, and they were so tall I had to crane my neck up to see the treetops. Their branches were so high, it was like they held up the skies above us.

Mick parked up on a small patch of grass littered with dirt bikes and other cars and turned off the engine. Our arrival had not gone unnoticed; several people were staring from outside a nearby house, and more than a few had stopped in their tracks.

Some of the kids were peering curiously, trying to get a better look at us. I waved at a small girl with long braided hair, and she smiled at me before hiding her face in her mother's skirt.

"Well," Penny said, confident as ever. "I guess we should find out where to go. Wouldn't want to miss the fun!"

With that, she opened her door and slid out of the passenger seat, landing daintily on her tiptoes so that her heels didn't sink into the grass.

I counted myself lucky: I had opted for simple flats for the occasion, as the invite had suggested. The ground was firm beneath my feet, and as I inhaled, the first lungful of cool forest air cleared my head, leaving me with a calmness that I hadn't felt in weeks.

"We're here for the... uh... bonding ceremony?" I heard Mick say to someone nearby.

"We have our invitation," Penny added, proffering a card identical to the one I had received. "Which way is the town hall, please?"

"Council house," a man corrected her, sounding gruff. His eyes were narrowed, and he stood hunched over with his hands in his pockets. Another man wandered over to the group and put a hand on his arm, and the first guy backed off immediately.

Huh. That was weird.

"Sorry about that." The second man addressed us with a warm smile, and we gravitated toward the friendly face. He shook each of our hands in turn as he spoke. "I'm Terry. The council house is right this way. I'll take you; I was just heading there myself, as are most of the others."

"Thanks." Penny smiled as we fell into step beside him. "We're not exactly from around here."

Terry laughed uproariously. "No kidding! Everyone knows everyone round here, just the way it is. Some don't take so kindly to new faces, but they'll get over it soon enough."

"We're friends of Allara's," Mick explained. "From the city?"

Something flickered behind Terry's eyes, but other than that his expression did not change. "Sure, of course! Our Allara's always been one for adventure. Loves new experiences, all kinds of people… Here we are." He pointed to a building, slightly larger than the others surrounding it, with a low, pitched roof. "This is the Council House. The center of our little community."

We climbed the steps and found ourselves in a room with a vaulted ceiling made from roughly cut logs, some as large as tree trunks. The ceiling held a light made from antlers, and the wooden benches were beautifully carved with leaping salmon, prowling mountain lions, and soaring ravens.

It was rustic, but beautiful. *Feels like home,* I thought.

Which was admittedly odd. I had never been anywhere quite like this before.

The room was already packed with what seemed to be almost every person in the village. With a shared look and an unspoken agreement, we chose a bench at the very back of the room and took our seats.

"Hey," Penny murmured, leaning in close to me. "Check out the eye candy."

I glanced over, following her gaze.

On the other side of the aisle were a group of youngish guys, sprawled out over the back benches and conversing lazily amongst themselves. Despite their casual demeanor, there was an alertness to the way they kept glancing over to the doors of the entrance that suggested they were keeping a close eye over the proceedings.

Almost like they're guarding the place.

But… from what?

This was a wedding, after all. Were they expecting someone to make a scene?

I didn't have time to wonder about what was going on, before Penny's elbow caught me sharply in the side. "Dibs on the cutie!" she whispered, giggling.

Which one is the cutie?

The truth was, they were all as good-looking as each other. I couldn't work out which one in particular she meant.

Even though they were all seated, I could tell they were unusually tall. They were broad, too, the width of their frames causing their suit jackets to sit almost awkwardly across their shoulders.

All of them cut an impressive figure, with firm jawlines, and white teeth that complemented easy, perfect smiles. Country living certainly seemed to agree with these men.

As I surreptitiously studied them, I noted their eyes ranged from a deep-set blue, through to piercing ultramarine, to light hazel. All were warm with good humor and made for a striking contrast against their deeply tanned skin.

For a brief, heart-stopping second, one particular set of hazel eyes met mine.

I felt myself flush, and looked away quickly, my heart hammering in my chest. I furtively wiped my palms against my skirt and looked intently down at the invite which lay in my lap.

God, it's hot in here.

I told myself I must have been mistaken. It wasn't like any of them would be looking at *me* for any reason. They were probably staring at Penny who was attractive and vivacious, and I just happened to be in the way while they were scoping her out.

I was too nervous to check and see if I was right. So, I decided to keep my eyes to myself from now on. There were plenty of other things to hold my attention, after all; up at the front, a group of musicians were performing a complex-looking piece that involved a pair of huge drums. Although I couldn't see much from my position, I was intrigued by the long, braided hair of the women playing the music and the long, sweeping robes of the elderly man who stood at the front of the hall.

"There's a buffet after, right?" Mick mumbled to Penny, who shooshed him as the music cut off abruptly and an eerie silence filled the room.

I watched as the double doors creaked open, and man entered through them, alone.

That was Reid, the man who had invited us here today in support of Allara.

I had a vague recollection of him; just a few brief moments when he'd stood in the doorway of our dim, smoky bar after Allara had punched the jerk who tried to hit on me and wouldn't take no for an answer. I'd only caught a few glimpses of Reid that night; what had stuck out to me most was his height and breadth, as well as the rough, battered leather jacket he wore.

Just like those other guys over the aisle. Just like the owner of the hazel eyes.

I forced my attention to remain on the groom—if that was what he was called, at a bonding ceremony. He was a lot more well-groomed than I remembered. His hair was combed, for one thing, and he was wearing slacks and a button up shirt that brought out the color of his eyes, which were just as piercing as all the others.

He made an odd gesture, crossing one arm over his body and putting his hand over his heart.

In unison, everyone in the congregation mimicked the gesture. After exchanging a couple of uncertain glances with Mick and Tammy, we followed suit.

Reid strode up the central aisle and came to a stop at the platform, just in front of the elderly man. The older guy looked like some sort of priest, but I didn't recognize the denomination of this church. His robes didn't look like any that I'd seen before.

The drums picked up again, and soon the entire room was filled with the sound. I could feel the buzzing through my feet, and my body unconsciously began to move with the music. I didn't notice for several seconds, and when I did, I continued. Those around us were also swaying, as well as stamping their feet in time to the rhythm.

The doors opened once more, and there was Allara. She entered, and then was followed by a few other women.

My friend looked completely and utterly radiant. Her long, dark hair was looped in a complex pattern at the nape of her neck; I knew she must have had someone else do her hair, because the Allara I knew would never have had the patience to fiddle with her tresses like that. She wore a simple long dress with embroidery around the sleeves and hem.

As she passed us, I realized that the design emulated the foliage that surrounded this place. The forest was echoed in her headpiece, too; the delicate silver band was fitted with amber pieces. Their golden hue stood out against her dark hair, making her look regal.

Once she reached Reid, she turned to face him.

And the look on his face at the sight of her...

I sighed, wondering what it would feel like to have someone look at me that way.

It wasn't that I didn't feel happy for Allara. I did. Extremely happy. I knew she'd had a tough time, and it seemed as if she'd finally found her place in the world again. She was back where she belonged, with her people, her family.

And she had this gorgeous guy by her side, who clearly adored her. Anyone could tell that he would do absolutely anything for her.

Now that we were on her turf, and I could observe her and Reid together, some pieces of the puzzle started to fall into place, but so much remained a mystery. Why had she rushed back so abruptly?

Was it only to be with this Reid guy? Or was there something else underlying it; something that fueled the strange watchfulness I could sense in many of the people around us?

Allara and Reid murmured their unusual vows to each other and the elderly man bound their hands with some kind of ribbon. The vows sounded arcane, almost mystical; like nothing I had ever heard before. He leaned in close to her to whisper something, and I watched her lips curve into a smile as she stared up at him with love in her eyes.

I couldn't begrudge Allara her happiness.

And yet, there was a not-insignificant part of me that ached with longing. They looked utterly content, like two halves of a perfect whole.

The beautiful ceremony unfolding in front of my eyes only exacerbated my feelings of loneliness. It brought home the knowledge that nobody would ever look at *me* that way. Never cradle my face, like I was something precious and irreplaceable to them. Never kiss me like they couldn't get enough, like there was nobody else in the room but the two of us.

I envied her the security of Reid's love, even as I celebrated for her. She knew the man she loved would never leave her or look at another woman. She knew that the love she felt was returned by her partner completely, and she had her whole community to celebrate this day with them both.

It was a life I would never know, and I was human enough to admit that it crushed me a little inside to acknowledge that fact.

Still, I held up my chin, smiling widely, and applauded with everyone else when Reid and Allara stood, their arms bound together, flushed and glowing with happiness.

It was a perfect day, and I wasn't going to let my private sorrow ruin it for anyone.

No way.